"That's how I treat my customers!"

Nicholas growled. "You've been making up stories about each piece of furniture you sell, haven't you? You've been—"

"Successful." Ali knew she was pushing him. His eyes glittered with anger that changed to heated desire.

Impulsively she rose on her tiptoes and brushed her lips across his.

He pulled her into his arms with a groan. Tracers of light spun crazily, a match struck to kindling igniting his repressed desire. The kiss was escalating when he broke away from her.

Passion had stripped off his mask. "Why did you do that?" he demanded.

"Because I wanted to."

"Do you always do what you want?" he asked, a note of condemnation in his voice.

"Always."

"You don't belong here." His knuckles were white as he gripped her chin. "*I* don't want you here." As if realizing what he was doing, he released her abruptly.

Ali smiled. "No. You don't *want* me here. But you do want me...."

Dear Reader,

"I just read *Forbidden Fantasy* and it was great!"

Your response to Tiffany White's last Temptation novel, #376 *Forbidden Fantasy*, was phenomenal. "I loved it!" was repeated over and over. As were the words: "Your warning label Red-hot was correct. It nearly scorched my fingers." "Wow!" "A keeper." "A winner." "Hot!"

Many of you gave the book to your husband to read, applauded Tiffany for capturing many women's fantasies and thanked us for publishing *Forbidden Fantasy*.

We hope you enjoy *A Dark and Stormy Knight* as much. Tiffany is a versatile author who likes to write a different kind of story in each book—this one is an amusing, sexy Gothic. She's been nominated by *Romantic Times* for the Reviewer's Choice Award, Best Temptation and for the Career Achievement Award as Most Sensual Author. Look for *Bad Attitude* by Tiffany in early 1993.

At Temptation we aim to be on the edge, bringing you sexy, daring stories such as our Rebels & Rogues miniseries. And don't miss the wonderful comedy of Elise Title's four-book miniseries, The Fortune Boys. What happens when you stand to *lose* an inheritance if you fall in love? Find out beginning in September with #412 *Adam & Eve*.

And to all of our readers who enjoyed *Forbidden Fantasy* and our other exciting Temptation novels, thank you!

Birgit Davis-Todd
Senior Editor

A Dark and Stormy Knight

TIFFANY WHITE

Harlequin Books

TORONTO • NEW YORK • LONDON
AMSTERDAM • PARIS • SYDNEY • HAMBURG
STOCKHOLM • ATHENS • TOKYO • MILAN
MADRID • WARSAW • BUDAPEST • AUCKLAND

For my friends—
Susann Batson, a writer who shares
my love of things fanciful, and
Nancy Dumeyer, entrepreneur extraordinaire

Published August 1992

ISBN 0-373-25507-1

A DARK AND STORMY KNIGHT

1

"WHO IS THAT MAN?"

Jessica Adams looked up from the paperwork spread before her to see a tall and blond young woman.

"I'm sorry to interrupt you," the woman said contritely, extending her hand. "My name is Ali Charbonneau. I was hoping you could tell me who Heathcliff is."

"Heathcliff?" Jessica repeated distractedly, her mind still occupied with the myriad details of running the estate sale. After shaking Ali's hand she glanced nervously at her watch and then at the people milling about in the foyer, library and adjoining halls. The stately old mansion was crowded with eager collectors and bargain hunters ready to spend their money *if* the auctioneer she'd hired arrived.

Ali's discreet cough brought Jessica's attention back to her as the younger woman nodded toward the tall, dark and handsome man who, now that Jessica considered it, did look as if he'd just stepped off the moors.

Pushing her glasses back up the bridge of her nose, Jessica said, "Nicholas Knight."

"But *who* is he?" Ali persisted.

Jessica looked at Ali then at Nicholas. He had opened one of the exquisitely carved doors of the huge fruitwood armoire in a corner of the library. A lock of his dark hair fell over his forehead as he bent his head to inspect its construction.

Jessica smiled. "He is a gorgeous specimen, isn't he? Almost worth the challenge . . . His mother and I were college roommates and Nicholas is my godson. But I'm afraid he's not for you, dear," she said, lowering her glasses and patting Ali's hand.

"Nicholas is much too—too troubled a man for such a sweet young thing as yourself." Satisfied she'd dissuaded Ali from the folly of pursuing Nicholas, Jessica moved forward to greet the tardy auctioneer.

But Ali was not the least bit dissuaded. *Sweet young thing*, indeed! Her father could have read the older woman chapter and verse refuting the impression of innocence that her wide brown eyes and blond hair gave.

She was a capable college graduate. So what if she'd graduated from a privileged women's college in southern Missouri. She had gotten her degree in psychology, hadn't she? So what if she had dabbled in dance, art and equestrian science first! A woman was entitled to change her mind. Besides, her major didn't make any difference to the future planned out by her parents.

She had a few months reprieve while her parents traveled Europe. Her mother was a genealogy nut, and her father's twenty-fifth anniversary gift was the ancestor-hunting trip. But when they returned Ali would be expected to join the family business, a chain of French delis. That job was just her father's way of saying he planned to keep his eye . . . and his thumb . . . on her. He wouldn't rest easy until his willful daughter was safely married.

Well, Daddy was in for a surprise. She had no intention of joining the family business to do busywork. And being *safely* married held even less appeal. While she fully appreciated all the benefits of her family's wealth, she also chafed at the accompanying restraints.

And so this summer she was going to show her parents they didn't need to take care of their little girl any longer. She was going to use her graduation money to set up some sort of business. And she wasn't going to marry until she was old enough to be considered a spinster—and maybe not even then.

But that didn't mean she was going to be a nun, she thought. A smile played over her lips. She watched "Heathcliff" continue to inspect the armoire. A scowl crossed his face. Too troubled, the woman had said. For herself, though, with her penchant for old-fashioned Gothic novels, he was irresistible.

To Ali it didn't matter that he looked like the cover model for one of those "Men who hate everything—but their mirrors" books that were always on the bestseller lists. Never one to let common sense get in the way of lust, Ali headed right for Nicholas Knight.

Standing behind him—Nicholas was still examining the armoire—Ali cleared her throat to get his attention.

He bumped his head on the frame of the armoire and swore as he turned to face her.

Ali winced and extended her hand. "Hi, I'm Ali Charbonneau," she said, flashing a smile. Her smile and the handshake wilted at the sight of the shocked expression that crossed his face. Not only did he not take her offered hand, he actually seemed to recoil.

Puzzled by his reaction but refusing to be put off so easily, she pressed ahead. "Isn't this armoire lovely?"

He grunted.

"You don't think so?"

Another grunt.

She crossed her arms in front of her, and couldn't resist asking, "Is that one grunt for no and two for yes?"

Nicholas walked away—no, fled, Ali amended.

"Nice to meet you, too," she said to thin air, taking a visual inventory of his retreating figure. His dark hair was straight and thick, grazing the collar of his leather jacket. Charcoal twill pants fitted him with tailored perfection. His shoes, however, were the most telling. They were loafers; soft, expensive leather loafers. In her experience they were the choice of aloof, arrogant men.

"Yoo-hoo!"

Ali looked around at the sound of the familiar shrill voice to see Caroline Farnsworth waving madly and heading her way. Ali had made her debut with Caroline at the Fleur-de-Lis Ball and the Farnsworths were in her family's social set. While Caroline was harmless, she had too much time and money on her hands—and, right now, Ali noted with a grimace, Caroline had her fiancé, Billy Lawrence, on her arm. Ali's friend had struggled through school with dyslexia and it had given her a poor self-image. That explained Billy.

"I told you it was Ali, Billy." Caroline bestowed a kiss-kiss greeting upon the air on both sides of Ali's cheeks. Billy took his usual furtive liberties. Ali ground her heel into his foot, smiling the whole time; she wouldn't embarrass Caroline for the world.

"Isn't this scene a bit musty for you?" Caroline asked. "What on earth are you doing at an estate sale?"

"I was thinking of getting Mother and Father an antique for their twenty-fifth anniversary. Do you think they'd like this armoire?"

"I like it," Billy said, looking not at the armoire but at Ali.

Ali shot him a covert glare while Caroline inspected the armoire. "It's in great condition and the carving on the doors is exquisite. I could coach you when the bidding starts so you don't overpay."

"I appreciate the offer, but I wouldn't want you to stay on my account."

"No problem. Mother said they had some antique hat pins, so I wanted to take a look at them for my collection. Come on, Billy."

"We'll be back," Billy said, winking over his shoulder while Caroline towed him through the crowd.

Glad that Caroline had left with bothersome Billy, Ali searched out her treasure. Nicholas had stopped to inspect a pie safe in mint condition in the hall off the library, running his long fingers over the decorative inserts in the doors.

Ali approached him again, elbowing her way through the throng of people milling in the hallway.

"I didn't get your name," she said, leaning forward to read the item number on the pie safe.

He closed his eyes and sighed with audible impatience. "What are you, a reporter?"

"I know," she ventured, amusement carving her lips, "I bet your name is Heathcliff."

"Heathcliff?"

"Uh-huh," she said, wondering how he liked being compared to a Gothic hero.

"Like the cat . . . ?" he asked with a raised eyebrow.

"The cat? Oh. You mean in the cartoon. No. Trust me, I don't find you even remotely amusing."

"Good. The feeling is mutual. Now, if you'll excuse me . . ." He turned away.

"Wait." She couldn't just let this fantastic specimen of manhood leave. She wasn't known as Miss Persistent for nothing.

He paused. "What is it now?"

"I was just wondering . . . What is it you do?"

He glared at her and Ali took a step back, the dark look in his eyes making her wonder if he was considering taking up murder as a new career.

"If you must know, I'm a dealer."

"Really? Used cars or drugs?" she asked, unable to resist baiting him.

"Antiques." He bit off the word. His eyes narrowed. "What was it you said you do?"

"I didn't." Ali turned away to join the crowd gathering around the auctioneer, who was pounding his gavel on the library table to gain everyone's attention. She didn't have to look behind her to know Nicholas Knight was watching her; the hairs on the back of her neck prickled.

A pair of six-year-olds were playing hide-and-seek between the wing chairs near the oversize fireplace when Caroline and Billy joined her. "You'd think people would have sense enough to leave their children with their nannies," Billy said, eyeing the youngsters with distaste.

"Now, Billy, not everyone is fortunate enough to have a nanny," Caroline scolded.

"Or wants one," Ali added, glad her own parents hadn't, despite their overprotectiveness.

As the estate sale moved along, the paintings were removed from the walls, leaving faded squares on the stucco. The last painting went rather quickly in a short but spirited bidding war between two elderly ladies who looked as though they might be close relatives.

"Did you find any hat pins you liked?" Ali asked Caroline, trying to ignore the continued effect Nicholas Knight had on the fine hairs along her arms. The man's effect on her was spreading!

"The collection is mostly junk," Billy told her.

"But we did find a nice deco diamond stickpin for Billy," Caroline said. "He's promised to spend the weekend at the lake with my parents if I buy it for him."

"How nice." Ali thought it was anything but nice, but kept her opinion to herself, having learned the hard way not to offer advice on friends' suitors, whether the opinion was solicited or not.

The furniture was next up for bid, with the pie safe being the first piece offered. The auctioneer set two hundred dollars as the opening bid.

"Two-fifty."

Ali recognized the firm, confident voice and felt her toes curl.

No one challenged his bid.

The auctioneer described the pie safe's perfect condition and illustrious history to no avail. Ali watched the two six-year-olds, now asleep on a wing chair in the stuffy room; the auctioneer began his "Going once, going twice" spiel.

No one was more surprised than Ali when she called out "Two-seventy-five!"

"But I thought you wanted the armoire," Caroline said.

"Three," Nicholas immediately countered.

Jessica looked a bit disconcerted at the bidding war that had erupted, but the auctioneer brightened, raising the ante. The bidding went back and forth a few times until Nicholas surprised Ali by dropping out.

"I don't know, Ali, I don't think your parents are the pie safe type," Caroline said, eyeing the piece Ali had bought. "Still, it wasn't a bad price, not a steal, of course, but at least you didn't overpay."

"I didn't buy it for my parents."

"You didn't?"

Ali shook her head.

"I don't understand."

"I bought it so he couldn't," Ali explained with a shrug.

"He?" Billy was suddenly interested.

"Never mind," Ali said. A lingerie chest came up for sale and the young mother of the sleeping youngsters was outbid.

The armoire Ali and Nicholas had been admiring followed.

"Five hundred," Nicholas called from behind her, his voice deep and sure.

The smug tone in Nicholas's voice annoyed Ali.

Taking a deep breath, she said, "Eleven hundred."

"I wouldn't pay a cent more," Caroline warned.

"Fifteen," came Nicholas's response.

"Sixteen," Ali countered. And just like that she owned an armoire and a pie safe.

Before she could consider what she'd done, the jewelry collection, including the stickpins, came up for bidding. Caroline pulled out her checkbook and frowned. "Oh dear, I've used my last check. I won't be able to buy your present."

An uncomfortable silence developed until Ali broke it. "That's okay, I'll get it and you can send me a check later," she said, when Billy made no offer to buy the coveted stickpin himself.

When the auctioneer opened the bidding on the stickpin, the young mother once again made an attempt to buy something she seemed to want very badly.

Ali felt like a heel, bidding against her for a jerk like Billy. She imagined the woman wanted the gift for her husband despite a budget strained by raising two children. But because she'd promised Caroline, she stayed in the bidding until she'd secured the diamond pin. After paying for it, she handed it to Billy, who made a show of thanking her with a tight hug while she fumed.

The estate sale started to wind down after the best pieces had been sold, and the crowd developed a greater interest in gossip than in antiques. A friend of Caroline's mother stopped to chat with Caroline about a charity affair, and Ali took the opportunity to explain to Billy that it would be a good idea for him to give the stickpin to the young mother who'd bid against her as a generous gesture.

When he failed to act on her suggestion, she resorted to blackmail, whispering she'd tell Caroline just what a sleaze he was. Caroline's companion drifted away to join her friends and Ali looked pointedly at Billy.

"You know, Caroline, I was thinking. Perhaps I ought to give this stickpin to the young woman who wanted it so badly. Would you mind terribly if I didn't keep it, after all?"

Caroline's face lit up. "Why, Billy, what a sweet and thoughtful thing to do! Isn't he just wonderful, Ali?"

"Wonderful," Ali agreed; the two of them headed in the direction of the woman gathering up her sleepy children.

Turning, Ali caught a glimpse of Nicholas's handsome profile.

She knew he'd been watching her covertly throughout the auction. *Yes, but is it me or my pie safe he covets?* she asked herself. Given his earlier startled reaction on meeting her, it was more than likely that he coveted her pie safe, she admitted with some reluctance. Perhaps they could strike some sort of bargain....

As she headed toward him it occurred to her she might benefit from her impulsive purchase by making a small profit. After all, she had no earthly need of a pie safe.

The trouble was, when she got a little closer, she saw he didn't look to be in much of a buying mood. His eyes held the dark, quiet fury of an approaching storm. Swallowing dryly, she went up to him, prepared to eat a little crow; it appeared he was going to be difficult. All thought of profit left her mind.

He spoke first, surprising her.

"So, you're a dealer too ... though not a very good one."

"What?"

"That is why you bought the pieces, isn't it?" he asked.

"I do hope you don't have any hard feelings about what happened," she said with a nervous laugh.

"Hard feelings. Hardly. It's business, after all. Even if you are a poor businesswoman."

"A poor—?"

"You overpaid," he said, his voice liberally laced with condescension, making it clear he didn't take her the least bit seriously.

"Is that a fact?" Ali asked with quiet fury, all thought of compromise—all sensible thought of any kind—taking flight. No matter how attractive this relic of superior masculinity before her was, he was a complete waste of any woman's time.

Nicholas Knight was clearly a misogynist. Why did men who looked like him always have to hate women? What had any woman ever done to him? And why did she have to have a penchant for setting men like him straight?

"Yes, it's a fact," Nicholas said coolly. "In the future I'd advise you to have a cooler head when bargaining. You do realize that after the pie safe, I deliberately bid high on the armoire."

Steam practically came out of Ali's ears. As it was, she felt herself blush furiously. "You deliberately—?"

"Yes, I wanted the pie safe. It's in remarkable condition and I have a buyer. After you overbid, I merely toyed with you."

"You . . . you . . . *toyed* with me?"

He nodded.

"Well, Heathcliff, I'm afraid you're going to find out you've *toyed* with the wrong person."

"Have I?"

"Yes. You see, I'm going to be the most expensive plaything you've ever had."

His eyes positively shone at her ill-chosen phrase, giving her threat a sexual spin.

She turned her back on him in an act of dismissal, her eyes searching out Jessica Adams. Nicholas Knight's words made her recall all the people who'd ever misjudged her. Her father immediately came to mind. He'd never understood her strong streak of determination.

Years ago in her childhood he'd said absolutely, definitely, she couldn't keep the puppy that had followed her home. But she'd shown him she could care for the pet and love it and had worn down her father's resistance.

Then there was Brad Davis, the class jock. He'd assured her he had the class presidency sewn up. By aligning all the nonathletic factions, she'd managed to eke out both a narrow victory and a date with him for the prom.

She didn't always reach her goal. She'd gone after the lead in the class musical and wound up in the chorus, but she did give everything she tried her best effort.

Locating Jessica in the crowd, Ali moved over to her. "Miss Adams, I'm Ali Charbonneau, remember?"

Jessica nodded, buttoning her suit jacket as she prepared to leave. "Call me Jessica, dear," she said with a friendly smile.

"Jessica. Ah, I was wondering. Is there some way I might arrange to have the pieces I bought delivered?"

"I can give you a name," Jessica replied, searching through a stack of papers until she came up with a business card. "This is the company I always use. They're expert at handling delicate items."

Ali took the card and hesitated.

"Is there anything else I can do for you, dear?" Jessica asked, putting the papers into her briefcase.

"Actually there is. Would you happen to know where Heathcliff has his shop?"

"Heathcliff . . . ? Oh, you mean Nicholas. His shop is in Stonebriar, dear."

"Stonebriar?"

"It's a small historic town nearby. Most of the homes there have been restored and turned into shops, making it a quaint commercial center for locals as well as tourists."

"Would you happen to know if there might be a shop to rent there? Something that wouldn't be prohibitively expensive. I'm considering opening a shop."

Jessica looked carefully at Ali. As if reaching an important decision, she said, "Yes, I do."

"I wouldn't be able to come up with much of a deposit to rent the shop," Ali continued, "but I would be willing to paint or whatever to help defray costs."

"Deal."

"Deal?"

Jessica offered her hand. "I own several small shops in Stonebriar, dear. And as it happens, I have a new one I'm readying to rent. It even has a room and bath on the second floor, should you want to live on the premises.

I'd be willing to forgo a deposit, if you're willing to do the interior painting it needs."

"Deal," Ali said, unable to suppress her excitement; they shook hands.

"Good. I've got an appointment scheduled in fifteen minutes, but I'll be free afterward. Here, take my card and come by later so I can show you the shop."

"Great," Ali agreed. "And Jessica . . . thanks."

Jessica watched her leave, aware Nicholas was also watching.

He joined her a moment later as she was picking up her briefcase to leave for her appointment.

Jessica smiled at him, undeterred by his dark mood. Her smile widened at his question.

"Who is that woman?"

2

"Here kitty, kitty, kitty ..."

Ali walked beneath the paint-spattered stepladder. A black cat had just wandered into the shop and crossed her path.

The cat, like Nicholas Knight, looked at her as if she'd crawled from under a rock and walked away from her.

"Nice to meet you, too," Ali said. She checked whimsically to see if the cat also wore the same expensive, soft leather loafers as Nicholas Knight, observing four white paws instead.

"I bet your name is Boots, isn't it?" she asked with a smile. "Either that, or you've managed to step in some wet paint somewhere."

Ali surveyed the drop cloths littering the floor of the shop she'd rented from Jessica. There was almost as much paint on them as there was on the freshly painted walls. Her schoolteachers' refrain echoed in her ears.... "Neatness counts." She'd never listened to them. For her, getting it done was always what really mattered, accomplishing something.

She had lots of energy and little patience. She preferred the excitement of plunging right in, heedless of pitfalls or dire predictions of doom. Thinking and planning were foreign to her nature. Instead she did whatever came to mind, trusting to gut instinct.

Besides, everything always seemed to work out eventually. Heeding the insistent voice of her conscience, she muttered, "Okay, so sometimes it doesn't."

But this wouldn't be one of those times, she assured herself. Nothing would go wrong—black cat and ladder notwithstanding.

She glanced down at the oversize T-shirt she wore over a pair of old black leggings. It bore the Nike slogan, one of her all-time favorite ad campaigns—Just Do It. Her feet were bare, save for the "white paws" she'd acquired by stepping on the paint-spattered drop cloths.

Giving up on coaxing the cat, Ali climbed the ladder to paint. As soon as she was hard at work the cat sat down at the base of the ladder and meowed, seeming to object to the ordinary name of Boots. "Too late now to make friends," Ali admonished the feline.

Dipping a paintbrush into a bucket of white paint with a pink tint, Ali promised, "But if you come back tomorrow and let me pet you, I'll see what I can do about scaring you up a saucer of milk."

The cat licked its paws, looking as if Ali's offer was beneath consideration.

Ali laughed and began applying the paint to the ceiling. "I see that tuna look in your eye. Guess you're right. It would take more than a saucer of milk to make *me* purr." Out of nowhere a picture of Nicholas Knight surfaced in her mind's eye and she found herself wondering what it would take to make *him* purr. . . .

Probably a woman of a delicate constitution, always on the verge of a swoon over his dark, intense, masculine presence. A woman who knew her place—somewhere near those sleek loafers of his. Someone who would probably even shine them and enjoy doing it. Unfortunately for him, such women no longer lurked in the attics of dark, brooding mansions. The sixties had come, along with the radical idea that women could actually think and do for themselves. She smiled to herself. Nicholas Knight did look as though he'd been in a rather bad mood since then when he'd found he'd been born decades too late.

She almost felt sorry for him; his mood was going to get a lot worse very soon. While it was clear to her she didn't have what it took to make Nicholas purr, she was quite certain she had what it took to make him growl.

She was going to prove him wrong.

So he thought she wasn't a good businesswoman, did he? His challenge was exactly what she needed.

If it hadn't been for her impulsive decision to open the antique shop, she would have procrastinated half the summer away, trying to decide what business she wanted to open. It had been her pattern in college to dabble in this and that.

Having made her decisions, and having ascertained that the shop was a viable business proposition, Ali had set about acquiring enough pieces to open the store. Though the recent articles she'd read in women's magazines had given her the germ of an idea about opening her own small business, as many women in the nineties were doing, it was Nicholas Knight she had to thank for making the decision easy by pushing her emotional buttons. Even though starting Ali's Antiques had been an impulsive act on her part, she *would* make it work. She was just as stubborn as her father, her mother liked to say. Probably because it was true.

Once when she'd been about eight she'd decided to take a new way home from school. She'd overheard another kid referring to it as a shortcut. Somehow she'd gotten the directions confused and had ended up getting lost.

It had started growing dark and she'd become frightened, but hadn't allowed herself to call home. It hadn't occurred to her that her parents would be worried and about to call the police until she finally found her way home.

They hadn't punished her, but they'd lectured her about acting on impulse. She hadn't told them about the new candy store she'd found. A neat, old-fashioned store she'd found by taking a chance.

A glob of paint splattered onto her hand and she began climbing down the ladder to get a cloth to remove the paint.

The shop door opened and Jessica Adams came inside. "I've brought tea," she said, holding up a brown paper bag.

"You've got great timing. I was just about to take a break and tea sounds wonderful," Ali said, lifting a paint-dotted drop cloth from a couple of folding chairs and a makeshift table consisting of two sawhorses and a door.

A black blur leaped onto one of the chairs and meowed, its yellow eyes surveying the fragrant brown sack in Jessica's beringed hand.

The older woman smiled. "If I'd known Nicholas's cat was going to be here, I'd have brought some milk with the tea." The woman and the cat continued to eye each other. "Strange, the cat is almost always with Nicholas . . ." Jessica said, her richly modulated voice trailing off. Then something seemed to occur to her and she asked, "Is he . . . ?"

"*Nicholas?*"

Ali rolled her eyes ceilingward. "Hardly. He thinks I'll bite or something. At the very least he thinks I'm a flake—he made that more than clear at the estate sale. Tell me, Jessica. Does he hate all women, or is it just me in particular?"

"I'm afraid—"

"No, don't tell me," Ali interrupted. "It's much more fun to imagine a background for him. Let's see…. I bet he's really a vampire, and he's in a real quandary because he's not used to modern women. If he bites our necks, we'll be around forever, and he much prefers an old-fashioned girl. The kind that didn't give him trouble. Alas, what's a thirsty vampire to do? No wonder he's so bad-tempered."

Jessica looked at her strangely.

Ali laughed. "Relax, Jessica. I'm only kidding. Besides, it was daylight when I met Nicholas...so he can't be a vampire."

Jessica appeared to be reconsidering the wisdom of renting her building to Ali, clearly not the least reassured by Ali's bit of madcap reasoning.

"So this is Nicholas's cat," Ali said, reaching out gently to stroke it.

The cat skittered off the chair, landing with a soft thud on all four white paws and stalked away, its back arched and tail twitching disdainfully. Jumping into the window facing the street, the cat turned its attention elsewhere, dismissing the two women.

"I should have known the cat belonged to Nicholas," Ali said. "The two of them have the same personality—or lack thereof."

Handing Ali a cup of tea when she sat down beside her, Jessica took a sip of her own. "Nicholas is all right, dear. It's just that he's . . . well . . ."

"Impossible," Ali supplied, then laughed out loud when Jessica nodded in feminine solidarity.

"That does seem to be the birthright of all handsome men, doesn't it, dear? My William was like that. He was six feet tall and his blue eyes matched his air force uniform exactly. Near to drove me crazy, he did. He's been dead these ten years and I still miss his ornery soul."

A smile lingered on her lips as she looked at the freshly painted walls of the shop. "The new coat of paint is a great improvement," Jessica said, taking in the soft glow of the pink-tinted white paint. "Have you decided when you plan to open for business?"

"That depends," Ali said, setting down her tea and glancing at the delicate gold and silver watch her parents had given her for graduation. "I've scheduled an appointment at four with the accountant I hired to help me set up the necessary paperwork. If he says everything is in order, I want to open this weekend, even though the contents will be a little sparse."

Jessica nodded. "Then you were able to manage to get the delivery company I recommended to guarantee delivery of the furniture."

"They promised me delivery tomorrow. In fact I've decided to take you up on your offer to let me live above the store."

"Are you excited, dear?" Jessica asked, smiling warmly and patting Ali's hand.

Ali nodded and flushed. "Excited, scared, nervous, you name it."

"You'll do fine. And don't pay any mind to Nicholas. It will do him good to have a little competition. He's become too set in his ways for a man in his thirties. I'm sure a smart young woman like yourself can take a bit of the wind out of his sails, if need be."

"How is Nicholas's business? I know there is a good market for antiques, but is Stonebriar big enough for the two of us?"

Jessica looked at her consideringly, a veil seeming to slip over her eyes for a moment. She apparently shrugged off whatever she was remembering. "Nicholas *is* a shrewd businessman. I won't kid you about that. You'll have to be on your toes to compete successfully against him. Business has been slow in Stonebriar because of the miserable weather, but things will pick up now that spring is coming. Everyone has cabin fever, and the first nice days always bring the customers out in force."

"I notice all the shops are closed on Mondays. Is there any particular reason? Is the weekend the best time for business?"

Jessica shook her head. "You'd think that, wouldn't you? It's not the case, though. You'll find the crowds are larger on the weekends—a lot of couples shop then. Most of your selling, however, will be done during the week, when women come back to buy the items."

"They come back? But why don't they just buy it when they see it? Wouldn't that be a lot simpler?"

"Simpler? Not exactly. You see whenever a woman spots something she likes, the man with her always says the same thing."

"What do you need that for?" Ali and Jessica chorused, then both laughed.

"So—you have a shop, too, or you used to have one," Ali surmised.

"No, a husband," Jessica answered. "I wouldn't like to be tied down to the hours owning a shop entails. For my part, I dabble in real estate and the occasional estate sale. Well, dear, I'd best be going," she concluded, getting up.

"So soon?" Ali objected.

Jessica looked at Ali's bare feet. "It's going to take an hour of soaking those in a bucket of turpentine to get the paint off. If you don't start now, you'll be late for your appointment with the accountant."

Ali wiggled her toes. "Nah, it's latex paint. It will all come off in the shower." Running her hand through her hair, she felt the rough dots of paint that had dripped from the ceiling. "But I guess I had better start getting ready since I have to wash my hair. As it is I'm going to have to French-braid it and wear it wet."

Picking up the empty containers and her brown paper bag, Ali carried the trash to the cardboard box in the corner that served as a wastebasket. "Oh, I meant to tell you . . . thanks for the sign for the shop. It's really pretty."

"You're welcome, dear," Jessica said with a pleased smile and moved to the door. "I thought the pastel oval sign with Ali's Antiques scripted in violet just the right touch to draw customers inside. Let me know if I can help you with anything. I know how difficult it is for a woman to start a new business."

As Ali watched Jessica walk down the street, a movement in the shop window caught her eye. It was Boots, swatting at a cobweb she'd yet to remove.

"Wait, Jessica!" Ali called. "What about the cat? Should I return it to him? Does Nicholas live above his antique shop?"

Jessica shook her head on both counts. "Just remember to let the cat out when you leave. Nicholas lives on the outskirts of town and the cat will go home when it's ready to."

Seeing the spark of curiosity in Ali's eyes, Jessica added, "Nicholas lives in the big old mansion on your left when you leave the south end of town. It's easy to recognize. It's the one with the tall, black iron fence around it."

Ali realized that Nicholas's cat and house matched him; both were aloof, foreboding and enticing.

She went back inside the shop and was about to put the lid on the paint can when she saw a spot on the ceiling she'd missed. Climbing back up the ladder, she began to cover the spot. She hummed tunelessly while her mind drifted to the mansion at the south end of town and its owner, the enigmatic Nicholas Knight.

"So this is where you've been hiding out away from me. Shame on you."

Ali nearly fell off the ladder at the intrusive deep growl.

She hadn't heard anyone enter the shop and for a moment was afraid she was hearing things or daydreaming out loud; after all, the owner of that very voice had been making the most deliciously wicked suggestions in her flight of fancy.

"What?" she finally inquired when she regained her power of speech.

Nicholas cast a disparaging glance her way. "I was talking to my cat. I passed Jessica outside, and she said it was over here at your shop."

"Oh, you're here for Boots," Ali said, putting up a hand to still her wildly beating heart and errant tongue, so she wouldn't tease him for being on the wrong side of town. Nicholas's antique shop, Knight's, was right at the other end.

"Boots..." Nicholas said, his eyebrow raised in what looked like consternation.

"Yeah, him—her—whatever," Ali said; a blur of black streaked past her.

Nicholas picked up the sleek black cat that was rubbing against his leg and purring with pleasure. As Nicholas absently stroked the cat, it continued purring. "*Her* name is Kashka."

"Kashka? I've never heard that name before. What kind of name is that for a cat?" Ali asked, tucking her long blond hair behind one ear after wiping a glob of paint from her hand.

"Better than Boots," Nicholas retorted.

That damned cat, who wouldn't give her the least bit of notice, continued to purr contentedly beneath the stroking of Nicholas's long sensitive fingers. Ali tore her gaze away.

"Tell me," Nicholas began again, his eyes surveying the empty shop littered with drop cloths. "Have you been planning to open a shop in Stonebriar all along, or is this some sudden impulse on your part, seeded by what I said to you at the estate sale?"

"Something you said?" Ali mumbled, making a pretense of trying to recall his words; they were, of course, engraved with embarrassing vividness on her mind.

"Oh, you mean what you said about my not being a good businesswoman . . . is that it?"

He nodded.

"Actually, I've been looking for something for a while now," she said evasively.

Nicholas gave her a hard stare that told her he knew he'd been brushed off. "Jessica tells me you plan on opening—ah, Ali's Antiques, isn't it?—for business this weekend. Is that right?"

Ali nodded. She wished he would stop stroking the purring cat.

"You need any help?"

"What?" Ali knew she hadn't been able to hide her astonishment at his offer. She eyed him warily, trying to gauge the meaning of this sudden turnabout in his until now less than charming demeanor. Her doubtful look brought an explanation from him.

"I thought about it and decided I might have been a little rough on you when we first met, okay?" he said with a shrug of his wide shoulders. The action caused his leather jacket to lift the hair grazing the collar.

His hair is as dark and sleek as the cat's, Ali thought dreamily, almost but not quite succumbing to his ready apology.

"*You* thought about it?" Her tone of voice underlined the serious doubt she felt.

"Okay, Jessica said—"

"No. I don't need any help," Ali cut in, seeing Jessica's fine meddling hand, stirring up a romance. She didn't need Jessica's kindly help with the unfairer sex.

If there was a guy with an attitude and a leather jacket within one hundred miles of her, she had the radar of a bat and would find him.

Unfortunately she knew she was also as blind as a bat when it came to that particular type of man. She imagined a car careening off a cliff to a crash-and-burn finale to make certain she wouldn't be tempted to succumb to Nicholas's fig leaf—er, olive branch. She shook her head. "Thanks, but no. I have everything under control," she told him, all too aware she was lying through her teeth.

"Look, I'm trying here—" Nicholas didn't bother to mask his frustration.

"Yes, and I know exactly what it is you're trying."

"What are you talking about?" he demanded, looking at her as if she'd just grown another head.

Ali looked at the cat Nicholas had just set upon the floor, then back at Nicholas. "I'm talking about industrial espionage."

"Industrial what? Are you crazy?"

Ali crossed her arms and smiled smugly. "Jessica happened to mention your cat is always with you, so don't you think it a little bit unusual that Kashka's over here at my shop . . . clear across town?"

"Let me get this straight," Nicholas said, raising his fingertips to rest them on his lean hips, the expression on his face incredulous. "Correct me if I'm wrong, but you think I sent Kashka all the way over here to snoop around and see what you'd tell her, is that it? This is what you're suggesting, isn't it?"

Ali shot him what she hoped was a pained look.

"Don't be ridiculous. What I think is that you dropped Kashka off here so you'd have a reason to return to retrieve her and snoop around the shop in the process." She couldn't believe what she'd just said.

Nicholas merely stared at her. "You're really paranoid." With that, beast and beastie stalked off.

Ali watched them go.

Paranoid! He'd said she was paranoid!

Wasn't that usually what brooding Gothic heroes who lived in dark old mansions accused heroines of being—right before some terrible fate befell them?

She continued to watch the retreating figures, wondering what her terrible fate was to be.

The worst destiny she could conjure up was falling in love with a tall, handsome, brooding man who couldn't love her back.

Someone like . . .

Someone exactly like . . .

Nicholas Knight.

JESSICA WAS WAITING for Nicholas when he arrived at his shop.

"She's a lovely girl, isn't she, Nicholas?" Jessica observed, ignoring his foul mood.

"Yeah, lovely," he said, his voice dripping sarcasm. "A real piece of work is what she is."

"You're not being fair to her, Nicholas."

"*I'm* not—?"

"It's not her fault she looks like . . ."

"It's more than that, Jessica." Nicholas shoved his hands through his hair. "I admit seeing her did strike sparks off me at first. But it's more than the physical resemblance."

"Nicholas . . ."

"It's true. She has the same determination to have her own way."

"She's not *her*, Nicholas."

He stared blankly into space. "I still want her out of Stonebriar. She isn't welcome here."

"Why not?"

Nicholas's tone was bleak. "It's too dangerous. What if it happened again?"

Jessica's words were gentle and soothing. "No one believes those old rumors, Nicholas. Let the ghosts rest."

"They won't. They won't ever stop haunting me."

3

FRIDAY EVENING found Ali settled in the quaint, narrow brick house she'd rented from Jessica Adams. The large room and bath above the shop were wallpapered in a tiny blue and yellow floral print. The paper was faded with age, yet still complemented the pieces of white wicker furniture she'd bought.

Finishing the last pages of the Gothic novel she was reading, she closed it with a sigh. Ali identified with Gothic heroines, even though they were out of fashion. Curious and impulsive by nature, she had never met a mystery she didn't want to solve and she did nothing by halves.

Untucking the soft quilt she'd wrapped around her, she decided to go downstairs to the shop to take another look, wanting everything to be perfect when she opened for business in the morning. Once downstairs, she surveyed her pleasingly displayed stock, her eyes resting on the pie safe Nicholas Knight had wanted. She hoped the buyer Nicholas had in mind would discover she'd bought it and come to investigate her shop instead.

Ali realized that she hadn't any idea what Nicholas's antique shop looked like. It was at the south end of town and it would probably be easy enough to find. She doubted he'd have a pastel sign like hers. He was more likely to have a sign with something like Enter At Your Own Risk written on it in Gothic script, she thought fancifully.

Glancing at her watch, Ali saw it was already half past four. It would soon be dark. All the shops in Stonebriar closed at four, so she wouldn't be able to actually go inside his place, but if she hurried she could peek into the window and get some idea.

As if she needed more ideas about Nicholas Knight, her conscience warned. He'd taken up permanent residence in her mind since she'd first laid eyes on him. And peeking into windows—really!

"Okay, okay, so I won't go," she mumbled beneath her breath, agreeing it was a bad idea as she walked to the pie safe and opened its door to display the perfect condition of its interior.

A moment later she was on her way out the door to follow up on her bad idea, lifting a sugar cookie from the silver tray beside the hotel registry as she passed.

When it came to temptation, her response was always to yield. Besides, what could it hurt to check out her only competition? It was a wise and sound business practice to do just that. Only when Nicholas did it was it called industrial espionage, she argued. She still couldn't believe she'd actually said that to him, but he was just the kind of man who riled her. She hated smugness. She hated good-looking smugness even more. If she had her way, she was going to do just what

Jessica had suggested—take the wind out of Nicholas Knight's sails.

Four blocks later she stood in front of Knight's Antiques. The round canvas awning over the door was a deep, dark green with the letters spelling out the name of the shop in white script. The shop door was made of thick, weathered oak.

Ali moved to take a look at the big display window. Its contents looked as though Nicholas had raided a Ralph Lauren warehouse. The display was masculine, moneyed and elegant. It had none of the warmth of her shop, but it did have a certain style, she conceded reluctantly.

She peered closer into the dark interior, her nose almost pressed against the window. She could just make out a pine cupboard filled with china and glassware, worn leather suitcases, and a cast-iron hitching post.

"The shop is closed," a deep voice said behind her.

Ali turned, ready to have her worst fears confirmed. Surprisingly, a perfect stranger stood before her instead of the brooding proprietor of Knight's Antiques. She let out a sigh of relief. It would have been totally mortifying to have been caught snooping around Nicholas's shop by him after she'd accused him of doing just that very thing at her place.

"I . . . I was just window-shopping," Ali stammered, finding herself making a hasty explanation, something she only did when she was flustered and feeling more than a little guilty. Any other time she would have stared down the stranger who had yet to introduce himself properly. Squinting, she saw what appeared to be a silver badge clipped on his belt.

"All the shops close at four," said the tall, fair man, who looked like one of Jessica's contemporaries, rocking back on his heels and studying her as if she were a very suspicious person.

Affronted, Ali hastened to explain. "I know. I have a shop here in Stonebriar myself. Maybe you've heard of it—Ali's Antiques."

"I don't think so, lady. I'm the police chief here in Stonebriar and I know everyone who . . . Wait a minute. You're that city woman Jessica told me about, aren't you? The one who's opening another antique furniture shop."

"That's me." Ali nodded and offered her hand. "Ali Charbonneau."

"Joe Allen," the man said by way of introduction as he took her hand. "Checking out the competition then, are you?" he asked, tipping back his hat and nodding to Nicholas's shop.

"Something like that."

Joe Allen's eyes were alive with curiosity "Does he know about you?"

"Mr. Knight and I have met." Ali didn't elaborate, to the police chief's obvious disappointment. She had a feeling Joe Allen was a prime source of the town's gossip, despite his badge.

"I see," he said, pulling his hat back down. "Well, you be real careful of Nicholas Knight. It wouldn't do to make an enemy of him. Rumor is it's not something you live to regret. Well, be careful walking back to your place, then."

"I'll keep my eyes open, Officer," Ali promised, annoyed by his warning. She was a full-grown woman, used to walking wherever she wanted in the big city at night. Stonebriar didn't hold any terrors for her. And what was all that nonsense about Nicholas? A person would think he was a murderer or something.

The police chief nodded and crossed the street to the town's restaurant bakery, Thomure's. When he went inside, Ali started back to her shop. She had only gone a few steps when she heard a meow behind her. Looking over her shoulder, she saw Kashka watching her in front of Knight's Antiques.

Glancing around to make certain the cat's owner was nowhere in sight, Ali called to the cat.

"Here kitty, kitty, kitty..."

The cat didn't move.

"Guess you know you caught me out without tuna, huh?" Ali said, shaking her head at the independent cat and grinning.

The cat's yellow eyes stared back at her unblinking; Kashka seemed to be not in the least amused. She meowed again, then turned and began to walk away, heading for the outskirts of town.

Ali frowned. Did that mean the cat wanted her to follow—or was it only dogs who did that? No matter, she decided with a careless shrug.

She wanted to follow.

Kashka was likely heading for the Knight mansion. It was a perfect opportunity to check out the place up close. If Nicholas happened to see her, she could pretend to be returning his cat. Since she'd already snooped around his antique shop, she might as well go ahead and take her curiosity to the limit.

It grew cooler and the shadows lengthened as she followed Kashka, who seemed to be in no particular hurry. But after about ten minutes she saw the ominous Knight mansion. Off to one side of the property lay the remains of what must have been a similar mansion.

"What are you doing here?"

Ali jumped, startled by the approaching male voice. She heard Kashka hiss, then an old man stepped through the damp, foggy mist that had suddenly risen, swirling its chilly fingers over the area. She relaxed, recognizing the owner of the model train shop in Stonebriar and his overweight beagle.

"I'm just out for a walk, same as you," she explained.

"A pretty young woman like you shouldn't be out here."

"For heaven's sake, Henry, don't you think you're being a little melodramatic? After all, this isn't the big city. I hardly think I have anything to fear in Stonebriar."

"I'm not talking about Stonebriar. I'm talking about *out here*." He nodded toward the Knight mansion while his beagle flopped down to rest.

"You mean Nicholas?" Ali laughed. "What, just because he doesn't like women? Nicholas's scowl doesn't scare me, Henry."

"Maybe it ought," he warned. "There's those who say he has a temper that takes over him. Those that say he ought to be locked up."

"*What?*"

"Just take heed and stay away from Nicholas Knight and the Knight mansion," Henry insisted, tugging on the beagle's leash. "Death isn't a visitor out here, but a welcome guest," he added cryptically and disappeared into the fog.

Ali shivered. To her right she could smell the nearby river. She pulled on the red cardigan she'd tied around her waist. Old Henry must have taken one too many hits to the head when he'd been a coach, she decided. Just because Nicholas looked threatening, Henry had him painted as some sort of deranged monster. *Small towns*, she thought with a shake of her head.

Through the drifting, shifting mist she saw the Knight mansion rise behind the tall black iron fence that surrounded the property. The once elegant building was set back several hundred feet from the street. It had the cold look of old stone and marble. Ali was surprised by its state of disrepair.

Somehow she hadn't thought of Nicholas Knight as having to work for a living. She'd believed Knight's Antiques to be a hobby he indulged in when he felt like it. After all, their sparring had played like some sort of game.

The disrepair of his home was in sharp contrast to the antique shop. Which of them represented the true Nicholas Knight? she wondered. The elegant, mon-eyed antique shop or the foreboding, crumbling ruin?

Or was he a combination of both . . . ?

As she stood staring at the old mansion, a lone light came on, shining through the gauzy curtain of an up-stairs window. She saw the shadow of a man walk in front of the window and recognized the figure as Nich-olas. The pool of light upstairs in the south wing was the only note of warmth. The rest of the place was en-veloped in darkness; an almost comforting darkness.

For whatever reason, she knew the Knight mansion was not a happy place.

Somehow she knew it held a terrible, dark secret.

Ali looked about for Kashka, only to find the cat had also faded into the night.

As she headed back to her shop something caught her eye, causing her steps to falter. She stumbled, but caught herself.

Had she seen something moving near the remains of that stone foundation? It had looked like a floating, ethereal figure in white . . . near a crumbling fireplace.

She closed her eyes and shook her head to clear it, but a low moan of a sigh carried on the damp breeze made her open her eyes wide.

Though she looked carefully, the figure had disap-peared. If it had been there at all.

Shaking off a shiver, Ali began walking again. Re-ally, she admonished herself. She needed to start varying her reading material if her favorite books were going to make her start seeing things.

THOMURE'S WAS BUSTLING with activity a week later when Jessica Adams stopped at Nicholas's table.

"How's the French toast?" she asked conversationally, watching him pour real maple syrup over the buttery cinnamon slices of thick French bread.

Nicholas grunted.

"That good, huh?" Jessica said and laughed. "I see you're your usual good-natured self, if a tad more moody than usual. It wouldn't be the success of Ali's Antiques that's the contributing factor to this morning's scowl, would it?"

"I couldn't care less about that Charbonneau woman," he lied. He wanted Ali Charbonneau gone in no uncertain terms and he was a man used to getting his way. But Ali Charbonneau had served him notice that she intended to stay in Stonebriar. He had been up half the night pacing, unable to get her tantalizing image from his mind. She'd rob him of his sanity if this continued . . . if he in fact had any left.

"Want to know a secret?" Jessica whispered.

"What?" he asked warily, lifting a piece of the fragrant French toast to his lips.

"It's the vanilla they add to the batter that gives the French toast its delicious taste. Joe said the cook told him." She looked at her watch. "He's late meeting me again."

Nicholas swallowed the bit of toast, washing it down with some freshly squeezed orange juice from a cartoon jelly glass. Though the food was elegant, the atmosphere of Thomure's was informal and fun.

"I think she's a witch," Nicholas said, looking up at Jessica.

"What?"

"She's a witch," Nicholas repeated with a careless shrug.

"What on earth are you talking about, Nicholas?"

"I'm talking about that Charbonneau woman. Kashka keeps disappearing over to her shop. Clients stop at my place, admire a piece of furniture and give every indication they will stop back by to make their purchase once they've explored the town."

"But what's wrong with that? It's a perfectly normal way to shop."

Nicholas licked the sticky syrup from his thumb, then wiped his hands on the blue- and white-striped terry towel beside his plate. "They never come back, Jessica," he said, tossing down the towel for emphasis.

Jessica chortled at his dramatics. "What are you saying? Are you implying our dear Ali is a serial killer? Really, dear boy, you take yourself way too seriously."

"No. I'm saying *your* dear Ali is a witch."

"Nicholas, really."

"We both know she overpaid for the antique furniture she bought. She has to overprice it to break even, much less make a profit. And yet her stuff is selling like…like hotcakes. She's a witch, I tell you. How else can she be stealing my customers?"

"I don't know, dear. Why don't you stop by her shop and observe?"

"I might just do that."

"Do what?" Joe Allen asked, finally arriving.

"Have you arrested for tardiness," Jessica chastised.

"It wasn't my fault," Joe said lamely. "Ali stopped me on the way over here to ask if she could borrow a broom. Seems there were some cobwebs she couldn't reach with her feather duster."

"*Her* broom was probably in the shop for repair," Nicholas muttered, shooting an "I told you so" glance at Jessica.

Jessica just shook her head.

"What was that, Nicholas?" Joe asked suspiciously.

"He said there was probably some room in the shop for repair," Jessica said, hastily redirecting Joe's penchant for baiting Nicholas and spreading gossip. "Ali moved in so quickly, I didn't have time to go over the shop like I usually do when I rent out a new property to a tenant."

"Oh." Joe looked puzzled for a moment. "Ali said the two of you had met."

"Yeah, we've met," Nicholas replied curtly, not taking the police chief's bait.

"Wonder why she was snooping around your place…." Joe said, clearly not giving up his search for gossip…old or new.

He had Nicholas's attention.

Nicholas set down his fork and pushed his plate aside. "When?" he asked, looking up at Joe consideringly.

"Let me think. I expect it was just about this time last week. I remember thinking she was a customer and telling her you were closed. She told me then she was opening a shop and that she was just checking out her competition.

"You know, when I was in her shop this morning I couldn't help but notice she'd just about sold everything in the place. It was looking mighty sparse, I'll tell you, and what furniture there was left mostly had Sold tags on it. I imagine that gets to you, doesn't it Nicholas . . . having a woman competitor? Wonder if anyone's warned her about the danger of crossing a Knight. . . ."

"That's enough, Joe," Jessica said, taking him in tow and steering him away. "I don't know about you, but I'm starved. . . ."

"Are you sure it's food you want? I don't have much time, you know," Joe said, clearly distracted by her flirting.

"I do love a man in uniform," Jessica said, and they headed for the door.

"I THINK I'M ADDICTED," Ali said to herself as she lifted one of Thomure's large sugar cookies from the silver tray next to the hotel registry. While the oversize sugar cookies were the best she'd ever tasted, it wasn't the cookie itself but the thin coating of glacé icing with a tart, lemony tang that had hooked her.

Taking a sip from her mug of tea, she studied the names written by customers in the antique hotel registry. From the various addresses she learned the visitors to Stonebriar were about evenly divided between tourists from out of town and visitors from the large metropolitan area of Saint Louis.

Stonebriar was made up of about five square blocks of restored, turn-of-the-century gingerbread houses, most of them shops. For the shoppers who came to visit the historic town it was like stepping into the pages of an illustrated fairy tale. The mansions lining the river on the outskirts of town were another sort of curiosity. They were more nightmare inspiring with their wild eccentricity, the privilege of great wealth. Their stone facades gave off an aloof air, and the ones in a state of disrepair like the Knight mansion fueled scary rumors.

Ali's first week in Stonebriar had been a success beyond her wildest hopes. Her eyes flicked to the dwindling pile of business cards next to the tray of sugar cookies. She made a mental note to replenish her stack of cards.

Turning, she let her gaze wander. Even if she closed the place down at that very moment, she would have shown the arrogant, aloof Nicholas Knight she wasn't a poor businesswoman.

But that wasn't the only reason she'd opened the shop. He'd only been the trigger. The main reason had been her desire to prove to herself—and to her father—that she could be independent. Even he would have to admit she had done well.

She liked being in charge and taking risks. In that way she resembled her father. Her more artistic bent came from her mother, who had been a model. A model who'd given up her career to make a home for the man she loved and their only child. But Ali wasn't like her mother. She wanted more.

It was the challenge every woman faced.

While Ali knew she would never be happy without something that was her own, the happy home her mother and father had given her made her want a family as well.

She caught her reflection in the mirror. Today she wore a soft peach sweater dress that complemented her tall, willowy figure. She'd pulled her hair to one side, catching it in a blond tumble with a matching peach ribbon. On her feet were soft ballet flats. The outfit made her feel feminine and sensual—and in a strange way, powerful.

There were only two items in the shop left for sale. One was the curly maple highboy and the other a camelback trunk. She walked over to the trunk and opened it to display its prettily papered interior.

She smiled, remembering a similar trunk. When she'd turned sixteen, she'd inherited the family heirloom from her grandmother. The trunk had been filled with silky, satiny lingerie her grandmother had had custom-made while in Paris. The pieces were some of Ali's favorite possessions. She often wore one of the camisoles beneath a jacket and loved the way the fabrics felt against her bare skin.

A sound behind her announced the arrival of two customers. The pair were obviously old friends, enjoying a day of each other's company. Upon seeing them, Ali figured they were browsers, not serious shoppers. They were probably out whiling away a pleasant day together, visiting the shops in Stonebriar and having the excellent lunch Thomure's was known for.

A challenge. Ali vowed the ladies were in need of a highboy or camelback trunk, whether they knew it or not. The camelback trunk, she decided, sizing them up. "Hello, ladies," she said, "I'm afraid I'm a bit low on stock at the moment. But I do have this lovely camelback trunk."

"Oh, we're just looking," they chorused.

"Of course. Try one of the sugar cookies from Thomure's, ladies. If you haven't had lunch yet, the restaurant has a taco salad on their lunch menu that's—"

"Spicier than a Zalman King movie. We know. We just came from having their taco salad for lunch. But I've still got room for a cookie, have you, Agnes?" the taller woman asked, reaching for one.

"Edith, would you just look at this old hotel registry," Agnes said. "We've got to sign it. After all, with names like Smith and Jones, we have an obligation to uphold."

Both women giggled like schoolgirls as they polished off their cookies and scripted Agnes Jones and Edith Smith onto the lined pages.

"You're both from the city, I see," Ali said, noting their addresses when the ladies moved to have a look about the shop.

"Yes, we're neighbors in the same condo complex," Agnes said, stopping to inspect the camelback trunk.

The shop door opened and Nicholas Knight entered. "Ladies," he said with a cordial smile.

The look in his eyes told Ali she wasn't included in the greeting.

Annoyed, Ali decided to ignore him. "I almost hate to sell that trunk," she said to the ladies.

"Why is that?" Edith asked, her curiosity clearly piqued.

"Because the trunk has a very romantic history."

"It does?"

Ali could feel Nicholas's burning gaze trained on her back; the fine hairs on her neck stood as they had during the estate sale auction when she'd bought the armoire and pie safe. Nervously clearing her throat, she drew a calming breath, then began her story of the camelback trunk's history.

"This trunk, ladies..." Ali said, stroking the rounded lid, "...once belonged to a pretty, diminutive Southern belle by the name of Caroline Savannah. It was an engagement present from her handsome, dashing fiancé, who was a cavalry officer—a *Yankee* captain."

"Really..." Agnes sighed, visibly entranced.

"They were to be married when the War between the States broke out. The wedding was postponed until after the war."

"Did they marry?" Agnes asked, caught up in the romance of the story.

"No."

"Why not?" the more practical Edith asked.

"Because the Savannah plantation was burned to the ground by Union soldiers. Caroline's parents called off her engagement to Captain Brannon and mailed back the trunk and engagement ring."

Ali ignored the strangled sound coming from the direction of Nicholas Knight.

"But didn't Captain Brannon try to persuade Caroline to marry him after the war, in spite of her parents' objections?" Agnes asked, plainly looking for a happy ending.

"It was too late. Along with the camelback trunk and ring they sent an announcement of Caroline Savannah's engagement to a wounded Southern soldier."

"Romeo and Juliet . . ." Agnes sighed again.

"Real life," Edith said matter-of-factly.

"But maybe it didn't end there," Agnes suggested, brightening. "It could have worked out, something might have happened so true love could triumph."

"*Hogwash.*"

The three women turned to Nicholas as one.

"Excuse me," Ali said, narrowing her eyes and flushing with indignation at his comment.

"You heard me," he said, crossing his arms over his wide chest and planting his feet firmly. "That yarn you've been spinning is nothing more than hogwash and you know it."

Agnes and Edith looked at each other indecisively, then back and forth between Ali and Nicholas.

Ali glared at Nicholas, then smiled sweetly. "Is that a fact, Mr. Knight? In that case, Agnes, why don't you lift the tray in the trunk and see what you believe?"

There was the tension of a standoff in the room. Agnes finally broke it by turning to lift the tray from the trunk to reveal something beneath.

"Oh my goodness!" she exclaimed, putting a hand to her chest.

"What? What is it?" Edith demanded, stepping toward the trunk to peer inside.

Ali lifted a Union officer's gauntlet lined with morocco leather from the trunk's bottom, along with a small rectangular card.

"Would you care to read the calling card, Mr. Knight?" Ali asked, offering it.

Through clenched teeth he answered, "I'm sure you'll read it to me."

Ali glanced down at the card and looked up at the two ladies. "Miss Caroline Savannah," she read.

Edith reached for it. "It's an old-fashioned calling card, how pretty!"

"I'll take it," Agnes said. "I must have the trunk."

"Will that be cash or charge?" Ali asked, shooting the righteous Mr. Knight a look of satisfaction.

He scowled and waited, cat for mouse, while Ali completed the sale and made arrangements to have the trunk shipped.

When the door closed behind Agnes and Edith, he advanced on Ali.

"Kashka isn't here," she said.

"I'm not here for Kashka and you well know it."

"Suppose you tell me why you are here, then—no, let me guess. You came to sabotage my business."

"Sabotage—"

"What you just did was not only rude, but sabotage plain and simple."

"What you did was lie plain and simple," Nicholas countered.

Ali put the sale ticket for the camelback trunk into the register. "You're being completely ridiculous," she said, shaking her head at him impatiently.

Nicholas closed his eyes in apparent frustration, then blinked them open. His eyes were dark and bright with anger. "Look, I know where you bought the trunk, I considered it myself. I inspected it very carefully, and that glove and calling card were not in the trunk when you bought it."

"So?"

He looked at her incredulously. "What did you do, for heaven's sake? Go and purchase those things and put them inside the trunk, then concoct that romantic drivel just to make a sale?"

"So what if I did?" she retorted, not the least bit repentant.

Then he was growling into her face. "That's how you've been doing it all along, isn't it?"

"Doing what? What on earth are you in such a lather about?"

"That's how you've been stealing my customers and talking them into buying your overpriced items. Why, you've been making up stories like that about each piece of furniture you sell, haven't you? You've been...you've been..." He was so outraged, he couldn't hardly speak.

"Successful," she supplied the word he was searching for. She knew she was deliberately pouring gasoline onto the flames of his outrage, but she also knew his anger was tempered by his breeding. He was royally frustrated, but wasn't really threatening her. He wanted to wring her neck, yes, but wouldn't. He wanted to put her in her place and fully intended to. He wanted... Suddenly she knew exactly what he wanted.... She saw...something as elemental as anger, and probably more frightening, in his eyes. She saw attraction, glittering heat.

Impulsively she rose on tiptoe and brushed her lips across his.

He pulled her into his arms with a groan, crushing his lips to hers. Tracers of light spun crazily, a match struck to kindling, igniting repressed desire.

The kiss was hauntingly poignant and wildly exciting, and was escalating when he suddenly broke away from her.

Both of them froze, staring at each other, dazed by the intensity and unexpected emotional involvement the kiss had exposed.

"Why did you do that?" he asked angrily.

"Because I wanted to," she answered flippantly, annoyed that he was refusing to acknowledge more than his anger.

"Do you always do what you want to?" he asked, a note of condemnation in his voice.

"Always."

"What are you going to do now?"

"What?"

"You've sold all the furniture except for one piece. You'll have to replenish your stock to stay in business. I have enough connections to make sure you won't be able to."

"Just because I sell stories with the furniture? Is that why I threaten you? Surely you realize people don't buy anything just for what it is alone. People are starved for a little romance." She considered what she had just said. "Is that what's the matter with you, Nicholas Knight? Are you starved for a little romance?"

"You're talking nonsense. If that's how things are done in the big city, go back there. You don't belong here."

His knuckles were white as he gripped her chin. "*I* don't want you here." Realizing what he was doing, he released her abruptly.

Ali smiled with a sensual surety. "No, Heathcliff. You don't *want* to want me here. But you do."

"Damn you," he growled and stalked out of her shop.

4

THAT EVENING Nicholas was a lonely figure moving through the darkness; he completed his three-mile run feeling anything but refreshed. His breath came in ragged gulps when he stopped at the big iron gate fronting the Knight mansion to collect the mail from the box.

Carrying the mail inside, he headed for the kitchen to quench his thirst with a tall glass of cool water and then began his aimless, restless prowl of the shadowy rooms. Finally, he went into the library and lit several candles before starting a fire in the hearth. Electricity was too harsh on nights like these. He tossed the unopened mail onto the table and sank onto the sofa, giving in to the ever encroaching mood of despair. Uttering an oath, he shoved his long fingers through his hair, hair as dark as his mood.

It was so very quiet. Too quiet.

Not peaceful, though. The Knight mansion would never be peaceful. There was no benefit to be gained from his solitude. It allowed him too much time to think . . . to remember . . . to *regret*.

Lifting his head and opening his eyes he stared bleakly around the room. His surroundings were wearing as threadbare as his sanity; the flames licking in the hearth couldn't warm his chilly soul. They only conjured up mocking images from the past, a shadowy land of intense pleasure and unbearable pain. The only sign of life was Kashka, stretched by the fire.

The mansion should be ringing with the sounds of laughter and grand parties. Instead it was crumbling into a ruin, mirroring his life. Its mistress should be a woman of flesh and blood, not a ghost.

Wild and primitive by nature, Nicholas kept his powerful emotions leashed, but he was growing very tired of living in the past with its ill-fitting constraints. The past held him hostage, and he could hear the clock ticking, ticking away.

It was a past that wouldn't stay buried, despite the graves in the local churchyard. Ghosts and memories both painful and pleasurable haunted the mansion and the surrounding grounds like guests who'd come to visit and stayed on, ignoring all hints to leave.

No matter how hard he tried, Nicholas couldn't seem to put the past to rest, couldn't seem to escape it's pull on him. He felt as if he would be forever bound by history, family and fate.

Jessica had always scolded him for being overly dramatic and for making grand assumptions based on very little. But Jessica was biased by her feelings for him. To all intents and purposes she had been his mother, filling in for his real mother whose health had been frail since his birth—a frailty that hadn't survived the scandal fifteen years ago.

And now *she* had come to Stonebriar. Just looking at Ali Charbonneau made the past alive again. She was, as Camilla had been, beautiful, headstrong and am-bitious. Yet despite the resemblance, or maybe be-cause of it, Nicholas felt himself drawn to Ali. He wanted to believe he wouldn't repeat the old mistakes. Maybe Ali was different.

No. He remembered her behavior at the auction when they'd first met, Ali flirting with her friend's boyfriend. That was exactly like Camilla.

He rubbed his eyes as if to erase Ali Charbonneau's image from his mind. "She's a blond witch," he mut-tered, kicking off his sneakers. Sinking back into the soft comfort of the sofa, he stretched out, propping his bare feet on the sofa's rolled arm. He shut his eyes, blocking out the sight of the dusty shelves of books lining the walls. He was so used to the neglect and dis-repair of the mansion that he no longer took note of it. But even with his eyes closed he could still see Ali Charbonneau's soft, pouty lips, could still *feel* them.

The refrain of an old song played in his mind.... "Bewitched, bothered and..." He swore again, ban-ishing the lyric.

He'd managed to keep his emotions under lock and key for the past fifteen years, had managed to keep his emotional distance while enjoying the physical plea-sures of a series of accommodating women who "knew the rules." He had decided long ago that there were some feelings too painful to be investigated or even ac-knowledged.

Now one brush of Ali's lips against his own had shot all those years of rigid control all to hell. Something in her kiss had called out to him—dared him to feel again. He didn't know what it was about her that reached him; he only knew it was dangerous.

For both of them.

He was the last of his family and was determined the family line would die with him. A wife and children were not to be for him. Odd, he thought, staring at the flames in the hearth, how what one was denied became the thing one most wanted in all the world.

In unguarded moments he'd found himself wondering what it would be like to teach a son to swim or watch a daughter at play with her dolls. And then he'd shaken his head at his out-of-step, old-world ideas about gender.

It would be nothing more than pure indulgence on his part to look into the face of his child to see his own features blended with those of the woman he loved. It would be a criminal indulgence.

At twenty he'd been madly, passionately in love with Camilla. She had died under suspicious circumstances. He'd been too young then to protect himself from the pain of the ensuing scandal, a scandal that continued to color his life. The townspeople still whispered about him.

He could have left Stonebriar, that was true. But there was a stubbornness in him. He wasn't a coward, whatever else he might be.

He reached for the crystal decanter of whiskey on the table. It had been a long time since he'd indulged, but tonight he had cause.

The library grew dark as the shadows lengthened after sunset. The somber room comforted him, and he poured a generous splash of whiskey into the heirloom family crystal. Picking up the heavy glass, he tossed the fiery liquid down his throat, then followed it with another.

Soon he would forget.

Forget the sweet, soft catch of surprise in Ali's breath when he'd claimed her lips.

Forget her seductive pull on his loins.

Because the one thing he couldn't afford to forget was that his family was cursed with madness—as Camilla had discovered too late.

The glass slipped from his fingers onto the once luxurious carpet, and he drifted into blessed oblivion, vowing he would not repeat his mistakes.

FROM HER WHITE WICKER rocker Ali contemplated the tiny print wallpaper. Back and forth, back and forth she rocked, her mind not on the characters in the paperback she'd been reading, but on Nicholas Knight. At that moment she could cheerfully have strangled him, poisoned him, throttled him, shot him, hit him over his gorgeous, stubborn head with a blunt instrument—whatever it might take to remove his obstinate opposition to her running a successful business in Stonebriar.

In the week since Nicholas had visited her shop and warned her he would put her out of business, he'd managed to do just that. Every single time she made a contact to purchase some antiques to replenish the stock in her store, the pieces would suddenly become unavailable. She didn't have to ask why; she knew. Nicholas had fulfilled his promise.

Why? Why did she threaten him so?

She had a feeling her impulsive kiss had threatened him more than her enterprising business. Why had she given in to her desire to kiss him? Hadn't she promised herself she'd steer clear of romantic involvement with men like him?

She shook her head and looked at Kashka, who seemed mesmerized by the flames in the fireplace. Why was she even thinking of pursuing a man who wanted to be rid of her? Or at least professed he did.

The kiss had left some doubt about that.

She'd initiated it to annoy him, and he'd taken the bait out of frustration, she knew. But the kiss had quickly escalated out of control. He'd pulled away from her as if he hadn't wanted her to know that beneath his veneer of aloof indifference was a passionate man.

They'd both lost their heads for a moment, had forgotten they were enemies and played at being much, much more than friends.

Well, she couldn't afford to lose her head again. Her goal was to convince her father that she was capable of leading her own life. It was going to take a clear head to decide how she was going to accomplish that now that Nicholas had thrown a spanner at her plans.

To distract her thoughts Ali picked up a copy of *Victoria* magazine and began flipping through it. She noted that calling cards were coming back into fashion, replacing conventional business cards. The article said it was because women had enough confidence to add their own touches to the workplace. She smiled, remembering the look on Nicholas's face when she'd read Caroline Savannah's name from the calling card in the trunk.

Glancing back through the magazine, something caught her eye and she stopped at a pictorial spread. It was of two young girls enjoying a tea party.

Suddenly she had an idea.

ALI SPENT THE NEXT several days using her family's business connections to put her idea into effect. A few telephone calls and a little rearranging and reinvestment of her profit from the antique shop were all that was required to put her back in business.

True, it was a completely different business from the antique shop she had originally opened, but most entrepreneurs tried their hand at several small businesses before they hit upon the right one for them. And really, having a different business wouldn't be such a bad idea. She and Nicholas wouldn't be in competition any longer. They could even become friends.

One thing remained constant; she sold the image along with the product in the Charbonneau Tearoom. True, the delicate sandwiches and dainty desserts were delicious, but their presentation on antique china tea services was the main attraction. After scouring the family attic and a shop in Saint Louis, Ali had decided to wear antique clothing. As an added touch she sold old-fashioned calling cards. In general she did everything she could to give her customers a bit of fantasy with their luncheon.

When she opened, her planning paid off handsomely.

Even her father would be proud, she decided at the end of her first few days of business. So far Nicholas hadn't shown up, but she had a feeling he would . . . if only to remind her the town wasn't big enough for the two of them. No matter; she intended to prove him wrong. And there was nothing he could do about it.

A niggling thought surfaced. Maybe there *was* something he could do about it. What if Nicholas really was dangerous? The police chief had certainly intimated as much with his thinly veiled warning. *Had* Nicholas killed someone? Was that why the townspeople seemed to give him such a wide berth?

She couldn't believe Nicholas was a murderer. If he were, he'd be locked up, wouldn't he? Whatever had happened must have been something he'd been blamed for that hadn't been his fault. Small towns had long memories.

So, it seemed, did Nicholas. Whatever had happened in his past still seemed to haunt him. Maybe that was part of his appeal. She wanted to make him smile— to laugh out loud. Or was she just desperate to gain his approval when he so clearly didn't approve of her?

But if she were honest with herself, it was more than his approval of her business skill she was after. She wanted—needed—Nicholas to acknowledge her as a woman.

She had, however, won over his cat. Now visibly enamored of Ali, Kashka was a frequent visitor.

"Come on, kitty, let's take you home before your lord and master accuses me of catnapping." Ali lifted the cat from her favorite spot in front of the fireplace, where she liked to lie and watch the licking flames. Kashka opened one yellow eye then closed it, feigning sleep. Not taken in by the old cat's tricks, Ali scooped her up and headed out.

The sun was setting as she made her way to the Knight mansion. Ali smiled to herself, knowing her excuse for a walk past Nicholas's house was as lame as a schoolgirl's with a mad crush.

"AWAITING THE ETERNALLY late police chief, I take it," Nicholas said when Jessica left her post at the entrance to Thomure's to sit down at his table.

"He has other redeeming qualities." Jessica picked up a fork.

"Uh-uh, no dessert before dinner," Nicholas said, shooing her foraging fork from the last of his carrot cake.

Ignoring his reprimand, Jessica nabbed a moist bit of cake with victorious relish. "Life is uncertain at best, dear boy. Eating dessert first makes perfect sense." Savoring the bite of stolen cake with obvious delight, Jessica then licked every bit of the cream cheese frosting from the tines of her fork. "This is delicious. I must have a piece."

Nicholas shook his head in disapproval as she flagged down a waitress and placed an order. "Oh, stop scowling at me, Nicholas. Really, you'd think someone with a sweet tooth like yours would have a sweeter disposition."

"My disposition is fine. I do believe that Charbonneau woman was beginning to have a bad influence on you. It's lucky she took my advice and left town."

"Left? Ali hasn't left town. Whatever are you talking about?"

Nicholas's scowl deepened. "I saw her taking down her sign in front of the shop a few days ago. I assumed she'd followed my suggestion that she return to the city, where she belongs."

"Well, she didn't. If you didn't spend so much time locked up in that dreary old stone mausoleum you call home, you'd know that. I do hope you've been spending your time there painting and not brooding."

Nicholas refused to respond. Jessica wouldn't stop hoping that he'd return to his painting. She continued to insist his early promise as a painter hadn't been a fluke, that his talent had been real and enduring.

He knew better. His first gallery showing had taken place a year after the scandal and it had been a disaster. The reviews had called his work passionless.

"I don't know why you continue to live in Saint Louis when you spend so much of your time in Stonebriar, taking care of business," Nicholas said, curious about

Ali's determination to stay. "Since you know all about what's going on, how is Ali's Antiques doing?"

"It's not. Ali closed the antique shop."

"I don't understand." Nicholas handed his empty plate to the waitress who brought Jessica's dessert.

"She's opened a tearoom instead."

"A—a—what?" Nicholas sputtered, nearly choking on the swallow of iced tea he'd taken from the pint mason jar Thomure's served it in.

"A tearoom," Jessica repeated around a forkful of carrot cake. "You know, I think it's the English walnuts that make this cake so good."

"A tearoom. What's she going to do with a tearoom? Read tea leaves?"

"Of course not, dear boy. You really ought to go and see it. Ali has a real flair and the luncheon is a special treat, something out of the ordinary."

"It's still the craziest thing I've ever heard. You don't just one day have an antique shop and the next turn it into a tearoom. Why did she do that?"

Jessica shook her head. "I don't know. Maybe it was the overhead. At any rate the tearoom is closer to her family's business—you know the Charbonneau French delis. Though I doubt it really matters much what sort of shop Ali has. She's quite a good businesswoman."

"And dense as a thicket. I made it more than plain to that woman that she wasn't welcome here. I don't want her in Stonebriar."

"We don't always get what we want, dear boy. And besides, you're being unfair to her. At any rate, it appears it will take more than your perpetual scowl to scare off the young lady."

The restaurant door opened and Joe Allen ambled toward their table, acknowledging a few patrons on the way. "Why, Jessica, you're already on dessert. I had no idea I was that late."

"You're not. And don't be getting any ideas, you're buying me dinner."

"Here, have my place." Nicholas rose. Leaving the two of them gently bickering, he paid his bill and headed into the night for the walk home.

A breeze drifted off the river, damp with the scent of early spring. As he walked he ruminated over the news that Ali Charbonneau hadn't left town. His first volley in what was shaping up to be a battle of wills had gone wide of its mark. Ali clearly didn't take hints, subtle or otherwise. There was no reason for her to stay in Stonebriar other than just to thwart him. She was being stubborn, pure and simple.

Leaving the shops behind, Nicholas reached the end of the street and turned down the road that ran along the river, where the old mansions stood like aging debutantes in a receiving line...some as elegant as they had been in their youth, others ravaged by the passing years.

Jessica had said his scowl was not enough to scare off Ali, Nicholas recalled. What, he wondered, would it take to scare her off? He was very much afraid of what might happen if she stayed.

Much as he wanted to draw her near, he knew he must push her away—far away.

NEARING THE TALL, black iron fence surrounding the Knight mansion, Ali sensed a movement near the crumbling ruins on the adjoining property. "It's a night creature, not a ghost, you silly goose," she admonished herself. But just as she was forcing herself to look away, she saw something move again.

Something white and floating.

Kashka meowed and bolted from her arms, disappearing into the darkness. Ali was of two minds; good sense told her to go home, while curiosity said, "Explore!" As usual, curiosity won out and she made her way to the remnants of what must once have been a stately mansion.

Pushing the tendrils that had fallen from her top-knot from her eyes, she wondered at the choice she'd made. What did she even hope to find? There were no such things as ghosts, were there?

She recalled old Henry's words of caution. And the shopkeeper she'd bought the Union officer's gauntlet from had warned her to beware of Nicholas Knight— warned her he was a dangerous man, a murderer. Ali had thought the woman a bit dotty. Perhaps she had been hasty in disregarding the rumors. At the very least she should have asked some questions.

And then there'd been Joe Allen's cryptic comments about *not* living to regret crossing Nicholas. . . .

Even Jessica had said her godson was a troubled young man.

No. She was letting her imagination run away with her. Just because Nicholas Knight was dark, mysterious and hated women, that didn't make him a murderer.

Did it?

She moved forward again, then stopped dead in her tracks.

Had that been a twig snapping behind her?

Before she could look over her shoulder, someone lunged forward and grabbed her, lifting her off her feet as she struggled.

Her bloodcurdling scream was cut short by a hand over her mouth. "I've got you now and whoever you are, you're no damned ghost."

The fact that she recognized the voice as belonging to Nicholas didn't reassure Ali. Quite the contrary.

"Let me go!" she demanded when he removed his hand, struggling to free herself from the strong arms that pinned her back against his solid chest.

"I've caught you trespassing on private property," Nicholas whispered near her ear. "I could have you arrested and thrown in jail."

Ali responded to his threat by biting his hand, breaking his grip to slip free. She turned to flee.

"Why, you little . . ." Nicholas tackled her, bringing both of them down to the rubble-strewn ground in a tangle of arms and legs.

"No! Get off me!" Ali pushed at Nicholas's chest, hitting him with balled fists.

Nicholas stood up but hovered over her. Ali got up, too, but found she was woozy from having the wind knocked out of her. She swayed dangerously, and he scooped her into his arms. "You shouldn't have tried to run from me."

Ali struggled again, but Nicholas only tightened his grip and started walking. Once Ali got over her shock, she found the experience of being held against Nicholas's hard, lean body. . . interesting. He entered the library through the open French doors and laid her upon the sofa.

Ali heard a faint clink of crystal, then he was forcing her to drink. Wine. It tasted like wine. Was he drugging her? she wondered in a fog. At the thought she tried to push the glass away, but he kept insisting she drink. In the end she did; her weakness was no match for his strength.

The wine she choked down had an immediate affect, leaving her feeling boneless, her muscles as slack as cooked spaghetti. She blinked and the room grew blurred. The sound of Nicholas's voice came as if from a great distance. She tried hard to concentrate, to make out what he was saying to her.

Forcing her eyes open, she surveyed the library as it came back into focus. Nicholas had left the room. Surely he knew she would try to escape. Why had he left her alone?

Where had he gone?

Think. She had to think.

He'd gone to get a weapon! He'd warned her to leave Stonebriar and she hadn't listened. Now he was going to dispose of her. The thought swept over her, and alarm pumped adrenaline into her system. Her heart began to hammer in her chest and she couldn't breathe.

A sound overhead caught her attention and she looked at the ornately molded ceiling. The unlit chandelier above her tinkled. She tried to stand, swayed on her feet and sank back onto the sofa.

Listening intently, she could make out the sound of running water. Was he washing away the blood of one of his victims? No, she was thinking crazy thoughts. The water stopped running and there were more footsteps, then silence—a threatening silence.

A breeze lifted a length of gauzy white curtain at the French door, then moved to make the candle flame on the mahogany mantel flicker. The dancing flame cast eerie shadows in the womblike room—a room that was meagerly furnished and, if the cobwebs decorating the chandelier were any indication, ill kept. If he killed her here, no maid would find her body.

She tried to stop her rampaging imagination, but it was useless; she felt as if she were trapped somewhere between Bluebeard's castle and the decaying ruin of Mrs. Havisham's wedding scene.

Surely Joe Allen wouldn't let a murderer live among the townspeople of Stonebriar? Even Jessica wouldn't protect her godson if he were a murderer.

Would she?

The footsteps above her started up again and she heard the sound of something being dragged across the floor. Could it be a body?

She had to get out, escape.

Looking around, she was startled to see herself in the large, rectangular, gilt-framed mirror over the mantel. No, wait! It wasn't her—it was the pale figure she'd seen in the ruins!

Sleepy, she was so sleepy.

Maybe if she closed her eyes for just a few seconds she could gather the strength to flee.

Drifting off to sleep she noticed the rosewood piano and found herself wondering why the inlaid keys seemed to glow in the dark when everything else appeared covered with layers of dust and neglect.

Nicholas came into her dream, bending over her, his eyes dark and bright. Did she see desire reflected there or was it menace? Was he in some sort of trance—had she been wrong about him not being a vampire? Or was he on drugs?

He began undoing her hair. She felt its weight fall about her face and shoulders.

His fingers inched up her skirt to midthigh.

And then he was undoing the top buttons of her blouse.

To her surprise, she didn't try to stop whatever he was doing. Instead she found herself watching as if from a distance, allowing him to position her against a soft mound of pillows while he lulled her with soothing words.

The tone of his voice enthralled her more than the words. In her dreamlike state she wished he would kiss her.

When he moved away, taking up a sketch pad, she felt oddly bereft.

FROM A DISTANCE, Ali heard someone playing the piano. The intensity of the playing gradually increased until the sheer force and volume woke her. Blinking her eyes, she slowly came awake, disoriented.

Where was she?

She looked around the room and her eyes collided with Nicholas's back. He was at the piano, his long fingers attacking the keys until the music reached a crescendo. His fingers stilled and he stared into the distance.

Ali looked down at herself. The top of her blouse was undone and her skirt was tossed around her thighs. She brushed a loose tendril of hair off her face.

It hadn't all been a dream!

Her movements alerted Nicholas. "So you're awake," he said, rising from the piano bench and coming to join her on the sofa.

She watched him, wide-eyed and silent.

He bent her leg to inspect the small, skinned mark left on her knees when she'd fallen, trying to run from him. "Does it hurt?" he asked, lowering his head and trailing his tongue over the mark.

She tried to pull her leg back but he held it firm. A lock of dark hair fell over his forehead as he began kissing the inside of her knee.

"I . . . I want to leave."

He stopped. "I've been trying to get you to do just that since you got here."

"That's not true. You kept me prisoner here in this library."

"Did I?" He ran his hand down the inside of her thigh in a caress that sent a warm ache to her core, eliciting a small gasp of surprise and arousal. "Little girls shouldn't come out to play with big boys. Why did you come here?"

"I thought I saw a ghost. . . ."

"Did you?" Looking at her, he allowed himself for a brief moment to believe she could help him banish that ghost. And then he broke her spell over him. Determined to push her away, to tamp down his dangerous longings, he gave her a look meant to chill her. "I suggest you take it as a warning and stay away," he said, pulling her into a bruising kiss. His hand slipped inside her open blouse to palm, then clench her breast in a display of barely leashed restraint. Pulling back from her, the look he gave turned brimstone hot. "Stay away, I'm telling you. The next time you may see a monster."

NICHOLAS STOOD at the French doors of the library, looking over the crumbling ruins next door. He'd just sent Ali away when he'd really wanted her to stay.

Still, he'd done what he had to do. He'd scared her off. She wouldn't be back.

And with any luck at all she'd leave Stonebriar sooner rather than later. He couldn't believe that having a shop was anything more than a passing fancy for Ali Charbonneau.

She was the kind of woman who toyed with things.

The kind of woman who left havoc in her wake.

But not this time.

Nicholas turned away from the French doors and the disturbing image of Ali.

CHIRPING SONGBIRDS serenaded Ali as she hurried home from the Knight mansion in the early morning hours. Her thoughts were on Nicholas's warning.

She thought about the haunted look in his dark eyes. And against her will she thought about the feel of his lips kissing the inside of her knee—thought about the punishing kiss and caress that had followed. Whom had he been punishing?

There was no way for her to be scared off by Nicholas Knight; she was way too intrigued...no matter what the danger.

And she was still intrigued later that morning when she wound down her horseback ride in Chesterfield, where her family boarded their horses. Monday had taken on a whole new slant now that it was her only day off.

She was surprised to find she wasn't sore after the fall she'd taken the night before in the ruins. Maybe Nicholas had magic kisses, she mused, as she urged her chestnut hunter over a low fence when they were heading back to the barn.

The hunter's hooves flew through a small stream on the other side, spraying Ali with water and making her laugh with the pure joy of an abandoned ride. Coaxing the chestnut into a canter, she imagined Nicholas in pursuit across a windswept moor.

He caught up with her in a field of heather. His laugh was pure male victor when he snatched her from her horse to his, claiming her as his bounty. Pulling up his dark, glorious steed he lowered both of them to the ground, startling a partridge into squawking indignantly.

Looking into her eyes, he pushed back the hood of her long gray cape with his thumbs, then traced her lips before allowing the ardor he'd reined in for so long full access to his victor's spoils. His tongue's thrust was possessive, all smoldering heat and sexual insinuation.

His eyes flew open in surprise at her response of wild abandonment, a response that fueled the urgency with which he removed her cloak and spread it over the ground beneath them. Pulling her back into his embrace, they slid to their knees in a quickly escalating kiss. Then she was beneath him, and when his hands slipped inside her clothing to touch her bare breasts, he lost the tether on his passion. His hands were urgent and insistent, his lips quickly replacing them, his damp caresses searing her with heat.

"Wait."

"Wait?" He raised his head and looked at her in puzzlement.

"I can't catch my breath," she said, laughing.

"Then I must be doing something right."

"Trust me, you're doing everything right."

"You're not," he countered, a teasing note in his voice. "Not that I'm complaining, you understand."

"What am I not doing right?" she demanded, tickling him with one of the pinkish-purple stalks of heather that grew all about them.

"Well," he began, inching up her skirt. "You don't seem to be a frightened damsel looking for someone to rescue you from this villainous victor plundering the spoils."

She pushed his hands away, shoved him backward and straddled him, pulling at his belt. "Are you kidding? I thought you'd never get here. Besides, this is my fantasy.... All you have to do is lean back and enjoy...and we'll just see who the victor is. And what was that crack about spoils?" she inquired, taking him into her hand.

"Ah...ah...ahhhhhh..."

"That's what I thought," Ali said, laughing out loud; she had the power to make the superior Nicholas Knight lose control.

Heading for the barn, she admonished herself without much enthusiasm that her fantasies really oughtn't to be so irreverent, not to mention politically incorrect. After all, they were innocent—well, maybe not exactly innocent. Reaching the barn, she dismounted and handed over the hunter to a stable boy, just as Caroline Farnsworth led out her bay.

"Ali, have you been set upon by a bandit?" Caroline asked with an uncertain laugh as her horse switched his dark tail and stamped impatiently.

Unlike Ali, who wore simple riding pants tucked into an old pair of tall black riding boots, paired with a white oxford cloth shirt, Caroline was formally dressed, down to black riding hat, jodhpurs and necktie.

"Yeah, a kissing bandit," Ali said, recalling her daydream. "You be careful you don't run into him. Billy's liable to break your engagement if you go and make him jealous."

Where Ali's windblown hair streamed from a clip at the nape of her neck, Caroline had tamed her hair into a proper roll. It was a shame that someone as particular as Caroline was going to wind up married to a snake like Billy Lawrence. Her friend, she suspected, was aware Billy was marrying her for her money. Sadly, Caroline's poor self-image had resigned her to believing that a man would find her money the most, if not the only attractive thing about her.

But Ali was fairly certain that Caroline was unaware of Billy's womanizing ways. Ali desperately wanted to warn her, but she'd made that blunder once before and knew it was a thankless task. Knew there was a very real chance she'd lose Caroline's friendship, as she'd lost her college roommate's, when she'd warned her that her new boyfriend was cribbing her work and laughing about her thick glasses behind her back.

Ali shook off the urge to tell Caroline, anyway.

"Haven't seen you around much lately, Ali. What have you been up to and what's his name?" Caroline asked as she mounted her bay.

"You're worse than Daddy, trying to marry me off. I haven't got time for romance. I've been busy opening my shop."

"Your shop?"

"Yes, I've opened a tearoom in Stonebriar," Ali answered, not bothering to mention the antique shop she'd tried first, because it might bring up the subject of Nicholas.

"Stonebriar..." Caroline said, tapping her riding crop against her chin.

"You know, it's that small historic town on the outskirts of the city. Why don't you come by for lunch and we'll talk?"

"I'd love to see it. I know, how about tomorrow? No, wait, I've got lunch with Billy tomorrow. Oh, but that's perfect. I can bring Billy along. It's a date, then. We'll see you tomorrow for lunch." Caroline's eyes twinkled, then she led her horse away, calling back, "Now, where exactly did you say it was you ran into that kissing bandit?"

Laughing, Ali waved, watching Caroline ride off, sitting her horse with perfect posture. It was going to be difficult to keep her mouth shut about Billy. Sometimes she was too impulsive and curious for her own good. That was why she was going to ask Jessica some questions about Nicholas—like was the gorgeous but troubled man really dangerous . . . ?

"HERE'S THE BOX of photographs. You can go through them and see if there are any you want to use." Jessica had invited Ali over to sort through the collection of Victorian photographs she was handling for an estate sale. Ali pulled out several suitable for the mood of her tea shop.

Ali had met Jessica in a small carriage house on the grounds of an estate full of the musty smell of age. The small space had held an elderly woman's lifetime of treasures. Ali wondered if one of the women in the photograph in her hand had been the elderly woman as a girl.

"You know, Jessica, there's a sameness to all these photographs. The women in them are lovely, but they all look so . . . so controlled. Their hair is twisted and tortured and rolled and pinned. Their clothes are buttoned and tied and cinched. Even their mouths are tightly held, as if they might say something wrong. If I had been a woman back then, I might have literally exploded from all the confinement. How did they stand it?"

"Why do you think they kept taking to their beds with tincture of laudanum, my dear?" Jessica asked.

Ali's eyes widened.

"Don't look so shocked, dear. Your generation didn't invent all the vices, you know."

The mention of drugs made Ali think of Nicholas and the wine he'd given her when he'd carried her back to the Knight mansion. She had since decided he hadn't drugged her; it had only been the wine that had made her drowsy. Her wild imagination must have taken over from there to inspire the dream. Still, she had some questions for Jessica.

"I've been wondering, Jessica. Was Knight Antiques a family business?"

"No," Jessica answered, sitting down in a wing chair. "Nicholas's father was a stockbroker and his mother a ballerina before she married. Why do you ask?"

"I'm curious about why Nicholas went into the antique business."

"He went into it quite by accident. You see, when he was unable to make a living as a painter, he began selling off the family heirlooms he'd inherited."

"A painter? Nicholas? Boy, that comes as a surprise," Ali said, taking the chair opposite Jessica, sensing the older woman was in the mood to talk.

"Why does Nicholas being a painter surprise you?"

"I know Nicholas is your godson and all, but to be honest, I wouldn't have thought he had the sensitivity to be an artist. A better career choice for him would be a hanging judge—he's pretty good at passing judgment."

"He's hardest on himself."

"Nicholas! You must be kidding. He thinks the world revolves around him."

"You're being too hard on him. It's been a long time since he's had any fun," Jessica said on a wistful note. Jessica removed her eyeglasses and rubbed at the bridge of her nose. "The thing about Nicholas is that he's too stubborn for his own good. He'd never admit he was emotionally needy, but he is."

"The only thing your godson needs is a quick kick in the ego," Ali said with a smile.

It was Jessica's turn to smile.

"And I think, dear, that you care just a little about my godson."

Ali didn't rise to Jessica's bait. Instead she pursued the subject of Nicholas being a painter. "What sort of painting does he do?"

"To my great disappointment Nicholas doesn't paint any longer. I keep encouraging him, but my words fall on deaf ears. It's a waste for him to run Knight's Antiques. But you can't make people believe in themselves, and Nicholas doesn't believe in his ability to paint any longer."

"Why not?"

"He was only twenty when he had his first showing, fifteen years ago. His first and only showing. It was a disaster."

"Disaster—that's a pretty strong word. Were the critics that hard on him ... were his paintings misunderstood?"

"The critics weren't kind, but there was more to it than that. The paintings in the showing weren't his best work. His best works were destroyed in the fire . . . the ones he painted before the . . ."

"Scandal," Ali supplied.

Jessica sighed and slipped her eyeglasses back on. "So you know about the scandal, then?"

"I've heard there are all sorts of rumors about the Knight family. . . ."

Jessica nodded. "It's true, the family does seem to be cursed. First there was Nicholas's grandfather's suicide. Then his father was rumored to have fleeced his best friend in the stock market. No one knows the truth of any of it. As to Nicholas and the fire . . . well, I'm afraid you'll have to ask him about that, dear."

"Okay, but tell me one thing—is Nicholas a murderer?"

"*Of course not!*" Jessica's glasses slipped off her nose in her outrage.

Ali thought then of friends and relatives of criminals who, when asked by reporters always responded that the suspect "was quiet, kept to himself and never bothered anyone."

Well, that description sure fitted Nicholas Knight to a fare-thee-well, except for one thing.

Nicholas Knight sure as hell bothered her.

THE FULL MOON shone silvery in the inky-black midnight sky. The man in the old mansion was torn; he paced back and forth in front of the window, occasionally stopping to look down over the crumbling ruin on the adjoining property. His pensive mood was broken only by one fact. Ali Charbonneau had said she'd seen a ghost. Until she'd made the claim, he'd thought he was the only one who saw the white specter.

Maybe he'd been wrong to scare Ali away.

Was it possible that he was wrong about her?

He moved back from the window to his work. Was he courting certain disaster by his actions? Could he be deceiving himself?

If he allowed himself to feel again, he was vulnerable. He knew it wasn't wise, but perhaps . . .

Stepping close, he stared at the yellow paint he'd put to canvas and dared insanity to come and claim him.

5

NICHOLAS TURNED the cross-stitched sign Jessica had made for him to Closed. He planned to make amends with Ali by having lunch at her tearoom. Noting with satisfaction that it was two o'clock, he expected to be one of few customers. With any luck at all, he might coax her into having lunch with him.

His last client had bought the cast-iron hitching post that had been in the shop since day one. Nicholas took the sale as a good sign.

His spirits high, he stopped for a bouquet of spring flowers as a peace offering.

A peace offering he ground beneath the heel of his polished loafer when he saw the red Mercedes parked outside the tearoom. He recognized the personalized plate... U-WISH. The Mercedes had been parked outside the estate sale, the day he'd first met Ali. He knew it belonged to the guy who had carried on the covert flirtation with Ali beneath her friend's nose. Was the gigolo here with his fiancée or alone, paying Ali an illicit visit?

After all, what did he really know about Ali? For the first time he considered her as someone separate from his memories.

He found her very attractive, but beyond that she was willful, as determined to have her own way as he was. Despite the fact that that annoyed him, he also liked it one hell of a lot.

She'd gotten through to him on a level where all other women had failed. Yet he couldn't control her and it bothered him. He was a man to whom control was a matter of survival. But perhaps it was time he began to open himself to risk.

Taking a deep breath while cursing his desires, emotional and physical, he cast aside his reservations and pushed open the door to the Charbonneau Tearoom.

"What are you doing here?" Ali asked, meeting him as he entered.

"Do you find that works for you as a greeting? I'd think it would drive customers away."

Nicholas watched Ali close her eyes in an apparent mental count to ten. He took the opportunity to make a quick study of her. She'd pulled back her long blond hair into a tidy knot at the nape of her neck, leaving just a few wispy tendrils framing her face. Her antique lace blouse had a high neck and she'd tucked the blouse into an ankle-length, narrow silk skirt.

Her look complemented the decor of the tearoom, which she'd given a genteel, old-fashioned air. The tearoom, like its proprietor, made him want to linger. His artist's eye appreciated her sense of style, while his masculine eye surveyed her soft curves.

Ali glared at him. "So are you looking for Kashka or just here looking for the usual?"

Nicholas raised an eyebrow. "The usual?"

"Trouble."

"Actually, I came to have lunch."

"You did?"

He nodded.

Glancing over her shoulder, he saw the lunch crowd had thinned out, as he'd hoped it would have. At the moment there were only two occupied tables.

The guy with the Mercedes and his fiancée were at a table for four by the window. Seeing that the creep wasn't there alone, Nicholas decided he might have been hasty in condemning Ali.

The two ladies at the other occupied table brought their tab to Ali and he waited while she rang it up and invited them to return.

"Why don't you join me for lunch?" Nicholas asked Ali as the two ladies left, promising not only to return but to bring their friends.

"I've already agreed to join Caroline and Billy. Come on, I'll introduce you to them and then we can all eat lunch together."

"Great," Nicholas mumbled beneath his breath with a decided lack of enthusiasm. It wasn't only that he wasn't particularly enchanted with her friends; he was disappointed not to be spending time with her alone. In a group he wouldn't be able to get to know Ali better.

Ali led him to the table near the window. "Caroline Farnsworth, Billy Lawrence, this is Nicholas Knight. He has a shop in Stonebriar called Knight's Antiques. You might want to stop by before you leave. I've asked him to join us for lunch since it's just the four of us, now that the lunch crowd has left."

"Nicholas, it's a pleasure to meet you," Caroline said, extending her hand in greeting while sliding a glance of approval at Ali.

"Miss Farnsworth," Nicholas said formally, only to solicit Caroline's shrill laugh and insistence he call her Caroline. Billy merely nodded, seeming less than thrilled with the idea of Nicholas joining them.

"Do you happen to have any antique stickpins in your shop?" Caroline asked. "I collect them."

"Not at the moment," Nicholas answered, picking up the menu. "What do you recommend, Ali?" he asked after scanning it.

"The chicken salad on croissant has been a big hit. Is that okay with everyone?" Getting their nods of approval, she headed for the kitchen and returned a few minutes later with a tray of sandwiches and a pitcher of iced tea. From the silence at the table it was obvious the three hadn't been engaged in friendly banter while she was away.

Billy was the one who finally spoke, condescension coloring his words. "So you're a shopkeeper, Nicholas?"

"That's right."

"And an artist," Ali added, setting a plate before Nicholas, who shot her a look of surprised disapproval. A look that said she had ventured into an area of his life she had no business knowing about, much less discussing with her friends.

"Really! How exciting," Caroline commented. "I wish I were a more creative person. I would love to be able to paint or set up a lovely shop like Ali's."

"But you're going to be married and have lots of babies," Ali said. "There's nothing more creative than making a happy home."

Billy covered Caroline's hand with his own. "That's right, darling. You'll have more than enough to do, just being my wife."

"We're getting married at Christmas," Caroline explained to Nicholas. "I've always wanted to have a holiday wedding with my bridesmaids in green velvet, carrying poinsettias for their bouquets."

"That sounds lovely. Congratulations," Nicholas said, though he felt sorry for her. Couldn't Caroline see what a jerk her fiancé was? He didn't know Caroline, of course, but she seemed nice enough, if spoiled. If his judgment was any good when it came to women, he thought with chagrin.

He wondered how Ali had found out about his being an artist. Jessica was the obvious answer. He was really going to have to talk to Jessica about her well-intentioned ways. Had she volunteered the information about him, or had Ali been prying? Just how much had Jessica told her?

"So how did your weekend at the lake with Caroline's parents go?" Ali asked Billy, interrupting Nicholas's musing.

"We didn't go to the lake. Billy had some last-minute business that came up. Mother and Father were very disappointed, but Billy's promised we'll go soon."

Nicholas looked at Billy and saw in his eyes that he hadn't any intention of going to the lake and spending time with her parents. "What kind of business are you in?" he asked, doubting Billy did much of anything that involved actual work.

"I'm an entrepreneur—I do a little of this and a little of that."

Entrepreneur...that could mean anything from bum to serious businessman to bastard. Nicholas wondered which end of the spectrum Billy Lawrence belonged to; he was damn certain it wasn't the middle.

Was that Ali's leg nudging his beneath the table?

He looked up, but she was the picture of perfect innocence. It must have been his imagination, he decided. No, there it was again. Suddenly he realized it was Billy, attempting to play footsie with Ali beneath the quilt-covered table with Caroline sitting right there. Hell, that was probably part of the kick for a jerk like him!

Was Ali receptive to Billy's attentions? She had seemed to be at the estate sale.

To be perverse, Nicholas slipped off his loafer and ran his toes up and down Billy's pants leg, watching him preen. He was just about to kick Billy in the shin when Caroline spoke.

"Are you married, Nicholas?"

"No."

"Oh, so then you're an eligible bachelor," Caroline said, smiling with encouragement to Ali.

Embarrassed by Caroline's well-meant but gossamer-thin hint, Ali changed the subject. "What do you all think of the chicken salad?"

"It's divine," the easily distracted Caroline said. "I love the green grape halves and slivers of almonds. Don't you agree, Billy?"

"Yes," he said, pushing back his empty plate. "Ali has just the right touch."

Nicholas felt like strangling Billy, knowing he was referring to the bit of beneath-the-table flirtation he thought he'd just conducted with Ali. He really was beneath contempt. Caroline didn't deserve to be saddled with a jerk like him, no matter how foolish she was. Why, he wondered, if Caroline and Ali were friends, didn't Ali say something?

"Are you ready for dessert?" Ali asked brightly, gathering up the empty plates. "I'll bring a fresh pitcher of iced tea as well."

"What do you recommend?" Nicholas asked.

"The caramel apple cobbler is still warm, and the walnut brownies topped with a scoop of French vanilla ice cream and hot fudge has been a huge hit."

"The brownie," Caroline decided, while Billy and Nicholas went for the caramel apple cobbler.

"Here, I'll help you with the pitcher of iced tea," Billy offered, picking up the empty pitcher and following Ali into the kitchen alcove.

"You're him, aren't you?"

"Excuse me?"

Caroline took a drink of iced tea and smiled at Nicholas. "I knew I'd seen you somewhere before. Yesterday I ran into Ali at the stable and I was surprised when she invited me to see her tearoom in Stonebriar. It wasn't until I saw you that I understood why Stonebriar."

"I still don't understand."

"You are the same guy who was at the estate sale where Ali purchased the antique armoire for her parents' wedding anniversary, aren't you?"

"I was there, yes."

"You must have done something that day to make Ali angry."

"I did?"

"Yes, she was in a real snit. Whatever it was, you certainly had her attention. You see, ever since Ali and I made our debut, she's had her pick of men."

Including your fiancé, Nicholas almost added, quickly asking exactly what she was saying instead.

"I'm saying that Ali is easily bored with most men. You must have intrigued her. What Ali really needs is a man who's a challenge."

"Really. Well, if you'll excuse me a moment, I've decided what I really need is some of the French vanilla ice cream on my cobbler. I'll be right back."

As Nicholas neared the kitchen alcove he overheard voices.

"Come on, Ali, you know you've been encouraging me."

"Billy, Caroline is going to come in here and catch you! Now stop it!"

Apparently Billy didn't. When Nicholas entered the alcove, Billy had Ali in an embrace.

"I think you'd better leave the lady alone," Nicholas advised menacingly as he yanked Billy away.

"This is none of your damn business," Billy said, jerking his arm free and stepping away to a safer distance.

"I'd say it's my business when you're mauling my woman."

"Your woman?" Billy looked from Nicholas to Ali.

"She sure as hell isn't yours. Your woman is wearing your engagement ring and waiting for you at the table. I suggest you join her there. *Now.*"

Billy considered Nicholas for a few fleeting seconds, shrugged and went to join Caroline.

"I'm not your woman!" Ali declared indignantly.

"So I lied."

Taking her wrist, he pulled her to him. His long forefinger tipped her chin, then he gave her a dose of her own medicine, his lips brushing hers in the same teasingly sensual kiss she'd given him that day in her shop.

He felt her pulse leap beneath his fingers. The fleeting kiss he'd planned escalated as he lost control. His hands rounded her hips and cupped her buttocks, the silk of her narrow skirt slippery beneath his fingers. He pressed her against his hardness, his mouth and hips grinding out a blatant and sensual message.

When he finally pulled away, they were both dazed. Ali looked every bit the disheveled Victorian virgin. More tendrils had escaped her sleek knot, her skirt was twisted, and her high-necked blouse had come undone.

Nicholas gave her a considering look. "Apparently you lied too," he taunted, turning to go, leaving the challenge hanging in the air between them.

"Why did you come back here?" she asked.

He looked over his shoulder and shrugged. "I wanted some ice cream on my cobbler."

"No, I mean why did you come here today?"

He leaned into the doorway of the alcove. "I came by to lend you a little encouragement."

"*You* lend me a little encouragement? Am I supposed to believe that?"

"You don't understand. I came by to encourage you to leave Stonebriar. It seems you didn't get my message the other night when I delivered it in person. Instead you opened this tearoom."

Ali shot him a defiant look. "Oh, I get your message all right. I'm just ignoring it."

"Tell me, city girl, why are you so determined to stay where you aren't wanted?"

"I could ask the same of you," she said flippantly, turning back to the dessert tray, dismissing him.

"Stonebriar is my home. My family has always lived here." The emotion in his voice surprised him, and he didn't care for the look of pity in her eyes when she turned at his words. "You don't belong here," he said, summoning anger.

"I'm staying."

"Not if I have anything to say about it."

"Well, you don't." She walked past him with the tray.

"We'll see about that." Scowling, he followed her back to the table.

THAT NIGHT Ali sat in her room above the tearoom, reviewing receipts. As she worked, she made notes about what was doing well and that wasn't, also jotting down new ideas.

The Chris Isaak song, "Wicked Game," began playing on the radio, luring her attention away from the task at hand. Nicholas came to mind, mouthing the eternal message, "Come closer, no, stay away." He sent out enough mixed signals to wreck trains from New York to Chicago.

She recalled his arrogance at lunch, especially when Billy Lawrence had somehow gotten the idea she was encouraging his advances. She could have handled Billy, but Nicholas had assumed the macho protector role, calling her "his woman." And then after he'd kissed her silly, he'd still insisted she leave Stonebriar. But his body had sent a totally different message. Was she going mad . . . picking up the feelings she wanted to believe existed where none did? Which was she supposed to believe, what Nicholas said or what he did?

No matter, she'd decided she was staying in Stonebriar.

She was going to prove to her father and to Nicholas that she was capable of holding her own against their wishes. No way was she going to allow the Charbonneau Tearoom to be anything but a success.

Gathering up the paperwork so she could get ready for bed, she was certain of two things.

Nicholas Knight wasn't going to shut her out.

And he certainly wasn't going to shut her down again.

EVERY MOLECULE in Nicholas Knight's body screamed for him to stop. Stop placing one foot in front of the other as he ran down the side of the blacktop road. Stop the pain.

He was soaked to the skin with sweat. Every breath he took fanned both the fire burning in his lungs and his annoyance. His long muscular legs were leaden from the five miles he'd already run, trying to get Ali Charbonneau out of his head.

The running hadn't worked. Nothing worked.

He'd planned to make amends with Ali at lunch, to get to know her better.

But walking in on her in a clinch with Billy Lawrence had put an end to that. He didn't need to get to know her any better. He knew all about women like her. He had learned from an expert when he'd been twenty.

And he'd paid dearly.

The only sound was the pounding of his sneakers on the road in the quiet night. A mist drifted lazily from the river and into town as he turned off the blacktop road. Up ahead and across the street was the Charbonneau Tearoom. He would have to run past it unless he wanted to make a tiring detour, which he didn't. The mist shifted and he saw a light still on above the tearoom. So Ali was still up, too, despite the late hour. He could hear the strains of a radio.

Was she having trouble sleeping, as well?

The mist continued to swirl, draping about him as he ran. It was like weightless cobwebs drifting in the inky night, revealing, then obscuring the shops.

Nearing the tearoom he slowed his steps until he finally came to a stop across the street. Bending from the waist, he braced his hands on his knees and took deep gulps of the damp night air.

As he stood there another light went on above the tearoom. He saw Ali enter the bathroom and take a bottle from a shelf on the wall.

She opened the bottle and upended it into the tub and he realized she was pouring bath oil. She was going to take a bath.

He could use one. A nice soapy, soothing bath. And a woman to bathe him.

He should keep on running. Run away.

Do anything but stay.

But he didn't. He didn't move at all. No, he continued his secret punishing vigil, wondering what she'd do . . . what she'd allow . . . if he knocked on her door.

She began unbuttoning her blouse and seemed to kick off a pair of shoes as she went down an inch or so in the frame of the window.

She was obviously getting undressed for her bath. It was time for him to leave.

A gentleman would leave now, he told himself.

To hell with being a gentleman.

As he continued watching, she finished undoing the buttons one by one. When she had done, she left the shirt hanging open in front but didn't remove it. She wasn't wearing a bra. He could see an inch of tantalizingly bare skin where the shirt didn't meet. There was a hint of the swell of her breasts.

He swallowed dryly. There was more than a hint of swelling response from his body. His damn traitorous body.

You're supposed to be tired, he admonished. *Dead tired.*

When Ali left the bathroom she was still wearing her shirt. She returned to his view a few moments later, carrying something frilly in her hands. He guessed it was something to sleep in. *Damn the woman!* Why couldn't she sleep in a long flannel gown instead of a scrap of lace that inspired his imagination? Uncomfortable, he adjusted himself, cursing his overactive and very lurid imagination.

As Ali hung the frilly garment on a hook he wondered if she knew he was watching her. Was she deliberately torturing him?

No, she couldn't know.

Could she?

He continued to watch.

Hating himself.

She knew . . . she was walking toward the window!

He swore at his stupidity and quickly dropped onto his haunches. Then he swore louder at the pain of a charley horse cramping his calf. "Ow . . . ouch! . . . oooow . . . ow . . ." Damn, but it hurt. *She was going to hear him.*

The cramp ceased just as she reached up and pulled down the shade, the action causing her shirt to reveal a quick flash of bare breast.

Sweet, soft, seductive, rosy-tipped temptation.

He let out a sigh. He ought to be relieved she hadn't caught him instead of disappointed she'd lowered the shade. He ought to be ashamed. He ought to go home. *Now.*

Turning, he rose to do just that and lost his balance when he ran into a fire hydrant. He went sprawling into the street, knocking over a trash can. The trash can was made of metal and created an ungodly racket, sounding to his ears like the crashing of a thousand cymbals.

No sooner had that sound stopped ringing in his ears than they were assaulted by another. "Me-ow . . . meow . . ." Kashka ran to him and continued mewing at the top of her feline voice.

"Shut up, go away, Kashka." Nicholas swore again, swiping at the cat who wanted to lick his salty body, minister to her master's wounds. Any minute now, Nicholas knew the shade was going to go up and Ali would find him out. She'd call Joe Allen and he'd not only arrest him but worse, tell everyone.

He deserved to be caught. But for once luck was with him and the shade remained drawn.

Dragging himself to his feet, Nicholas picked up the cat, restrained himself from strangling Kashka when she kept mewing as if she were being killed and limped the rest of the way home.

He let Kashka down in the kitchen, then went upstairs to the south wing, carrying a bucket of ice, an apple and a knife.

Setting the ice bucket upon the floor next to a wooden stool, he dropped the apple and knife on top of the ice. Then reaching up and crossing his arms behind his head, he pulled off his sweat-soaked tank. Rolling it into a ball, he wiped it across his chest and tossed it into a corner.

He stopped to light a candle, not wanting the brightness of electricity. Eerie shadows flickered on the walls and danced in the moonlight.

Lowering himself to the wooden stool, he dipped his hand into the bucket of ice and rubbed a handful over his hot, sweaty body. He repeated the action several times. He stopped when he noticed an abrasion on his leg where he'd fallen.

Seeing the mark brought his mind back to Ali and her skinned knee.

Damn, but he hated these nights. Nights when the mist rose off the river to swirl around the damp stone walls of the Knight mansion, when the specter in white walked.

The moon was visible through the window, a diamond crescent in a black satin sky. It was *her* kind of night. He didn't have the strength to go to the window to see if she roamed the crumbling ruins...or so he told himself.

He'd almost been foolish today. How Camilla would have laughed at his romantic soul, his belief that Ali was different. His belief that maybe he and Ali had a chance.

He sat on a stool . . . a nearly naked knight in black nylon running shorts, peeling the apple he'd retrieved from the ice bucket. The moonlight glinted off the knife as he stared at the canvas before him.

He had to get rid of her.

Before the madness came.

6

DESPITE HER DIFFICULTY in falling asleep the night before, nine o'clock found Ali not only awake and up but
back from a leisurely walk picking wildflowers for the
tearoom.

The long soak she'd had in the tub the night before
had loosened the kinks in her body, and the ones in her
mind, as well. She'd decided she was not about to let
Nicholas's perpetual threats continue to bother her.

Nothing could spoil the good mood she was in.

The tearoom was doing even better than she might
have hoped. When her parents returned from Europe,
her father would see at last that she was a grown
woman, capable of running her own life, and not the
little girl who continually strove to please him.

A powerful businessman, her father was a dictator
in his personal life. A benevolent dictator, but a dictator nonetheless. He expected his family to do his bidding, no questions asked or opinions expressed.

Though she loved him, he was the reason Ali looked
with such a jaundiced eye at the institution of marriage. It didn't surprise her at all that recent surveys had
shown marriage was healthier for men than women.
Her mother had a good life, it was true, but she didn't
have much in the way of personal freedom or expres-

sion. She was *Mrs.* Charbonneau, and her life revolved around her husband's wishes. There was no such thing as equality in her parents' marriage.

And it was just the sort of marriage her father had planned for her, Ali knew. When he returned from Europe and saw how well her tearoom was doing, maybe he would finally understand she was having none of his plans.

When she heard someone knocking at the door, her gaze flew to the clock on the wall. Had her daydreaming gone on longer than she'd realized? Surely it couldn't be time to open. She let out a sigh of relief when she saw that it was only nine-thirty.

"We're not open for business yet," she called from the kitchen alcove, knowing full well she couldn't be heard. She figured when no one answered the door, whoever it was would go away and return later.

The knocking continued.

Ali stopped putting the fresh flowers into small vases for the tables and went to explain the hours of the tearoom to her caller. She straightened one of the Victorian pictures Jessica had found for her. She'd had them framed in antique silver and had hung them in an arrangement near the front door, above the hotel register that she'd kept for her guests to sign.

When she opened the door, Kashka darted inside, so she half expected to see the cat's brooding master standing there to ruin her day. But it wasn't him. It was a compact, redheaded woman in a black suit instead.

"I'm sorry, but we aren't open for lunch until eleven," Ali explained.

"I know. I'm not here for lunch. I'd like to come inside and talk with you."

"Oh." Then Ali noticed the woman was wearing a badge on her jacket and carrying some sort of paperwork on a clipboard in her hand. She must be taking some sort of survey.

Offering her hand, the woman smiled. "I'm Mrs. Dash from the Jefferson County Health Department. And you, I assume, are the owner of this shop."

"Yes," Ali answered, not liking the feeling she was getting in the pit of her stomach.

"Good, then you're the person I need to talk with. May I come inside?"

Ali stood aside, allowing her to enter. "Who sent you?" she asked the woman, knowing the answer. So much for her good mood.

"We got a complaint that someone became ill after eating in the tearoom."

"Let me guess who," Ali muttered beneath her breath.

"What's that?" the woman asked, rising on tiptoe to study the antique pictures.

"I was wondering if you could give me an idea of who that someone might be. It's something someone with a grudge might do, don't you agree?"

The woman turned her attention back to Ali and nodded. "That's always a possibility, of course. We do get a certain amount of that sort of thing. I'm sorry, but we have to check out every complaint to see if it has any merit."

"Well, you won't be finding any bugs here." Ali cast a glance at Kashka curled near the fireplace, watching the fire. "No mice, either."

"I should hope not. Your shop looks lovely. I wouldn't worry, but I do have a checklist of things I must go through."

"A checklist?" Ali's stomach turned.

"Yes. Each item on the list has a scoring point. Anyone who is unlucky enough to get under seventy points gets closed down, I'm afraid."

"I'm not worried about you closing me down," Ali said with more confidence than she felt.

"Good, then I'll just have a look around," the woman said, her brown eyes already taking inventory. "I'll let you know when I've completed the inspection."

Ali went back to the kitchen alcove and quickly finished her task. When she had the vases all ready, she carried them to the tables. The woman went to the kitchen alcove and Ali moved to the fireplace to stroke Kashka and think black thoughts about the cat's owner. It appeared there was nothing he wouldn't stoop to, just to get his own way.

In about twenty minutes Mrs. Dash had completed her inspection and approached Ali. "The place is spotless."

"Good, then there's no problem."

The woman looked genuinely sorry. "Not exactly. I'm afraid you do have some problem areas."

"I do? I thought you said it was spotless...and I have my merchant's license and my restaurant license."

"Yes, I know you do." The woman nodded in agreement. "But there's still a problem."

"Oh you mean the cat. She's not mine. She just comes by sometimes."

"Actually I was talking about the sink in the kitchen. That's a problem."

"It is?"

"You need three sinks, not one," Mrs. Dash said, looking up at her from her list.

"*Three?*"

"And where have your guests been going for a rest room?"

"Next door," Ali supplied. "No one's here for very long. It's just a tearoom."

"You'll have to have a rest room and add two sinks. I'm sorry, but that's the law. You have thirty days to make the changes, or your restaurant license will be revoked by the Health Department, closing you down."

"I see," Ali said, choking back threatening tears.

"I'll leave a copy of the report with you. I'm sure you'll work things out."

Patting Ali's hand in a show of concern, the woman left, taking with her any remnants of Ali's earlier good mood.

She wiped the back of her hand across her eyes, angry at her tears. Angry at him.

Going to the fireplace, she added a log to the fire, causing an ember to pop onto the hearth. Kashka swiped a paw at it and Ali shooed her away. Kashka meowed and stalked to the front window. After replacing the fire screen, Ali followed Kashka to the window. She stood there looking out, watching the gentle raindrops splash against the windowpane.

She sniffed back a sob. Nicholas had closed her down again. Well, she was down, but she wasn't out. She'd even open a new business if she had to, though she had no earthly idea what it might be.

After the luncheon crowd had gone, she'd scanned the local newspaper, searching for ideas. The Stonebriar Historical Society monthly meeting was a heaven-sent opportunity. If she went to the meeting, she might come up with an idea for a shop that would withstand Nicholas's dogged attempts to get her out of Stonebriar.

THAT EVENING as Ali entered the lovely old church that had been donated for the headquarters of the Stonebriar Historical Society, she wondered what Nicholas would think about what she was doing. He probably believed she'd packed her bags and gone after his little stunt of sending out the Health Department. Unfortunately for him, he'd failed to take account of her stubborn streak, the one her mother claimed she got from her father.

She might even find out from the ladies of the society why he wanted her gone so desperately—surely the group harbored a town gossip or two?

She headed down the row of polished pews, smiling in satisfaction. The smile froze on her lips when she saw who was sitting to one side of the gathering.

What was *he* doing here?

Her only comfort was that Nicholas seemed equally surprised to see her. She slipped into a pew just as the chairwoman brought the chatting group to order.

The time crawled by while they discussed the pros and cons of buying an old house to add to the ones they'd restored for the house tour that was held every Tuesday.

And then they discussed paving the road, which seemed to be an ongoing battle between two pretty evenly divided groups. The whole while Ali could feel Nicholas's eyes on her.

It was getting late and Ali was beginning to doubt the wisdom of her idea, when the chairwoman finally opened the meeting to general questions.

Ali raised her hand and the chairwoman called on her. She stood, carefully averting her eyes from Nicholas and began to speak. "I was paid a visit by the Health Department this morning, and it seems I would need to make a lot of expensive changes to my tearoom to be able to stay in business. I've decided, therefore, to close the tearoom in favor of opening a shop that doesn't have the stringent requirements for serving food. Do any of you ladies or gentlemen—" she turned and stared directly at Nicholas "—have any suggestions?"

"You might try opening something that isn't in direct competition with the shops already here," Nicholas opined.

"Such as?"

"I know. How about a sculptured-nail shop?" an elegant lady in red with long, scarlet nails suggested. "The nail shop where I get mine done is in the city. It would be so convenient to have one here in town."

"We don't want anything that contemporary here. We want to keep Stonebriar's historic setting," Nicholas insisted.

"How about a baseball-card shop?" Old Henry, the retired coach who owned the model-train shop, suggested.

"Still too modern," Nicholas objected. "Besides, I doubt she knows anything about baseball, Henry."

"Then maybe a flower shop," an elderly lady in purple proposed, smiling sweetly at Ali.

"We already have one," Nicholas said, looking at Ali with the light of victory in his dark eyes.

Ali glared at him. "I only hear you objecting, Mr. Knight. Don't you have any suggestions?"

"Would you like me to make one?"

She was sure she wouldn't and sure she already knew what it was...leave town. But she wasn't about to back down. "If you'd like to make a suggestion, I would certainly be willing to entertain it."

She could tell he hadn't been ready for that. There was a long silence as the group waited expectantly for his idea.

"You could open a dressmaking shop," he said finally.

"A dressmaking shop?"

Nicholas nodded. "I'm sure some of the ladies here would be happy to help you locate turn-of-the-century patterns."

"I can't sew," Ali said, thinking *he* was a turn-of-the-century pattern.

"Really? Tell us, Ms. Charbonneau, what is it that you know how to do?"

"Treat people well," she shot back.

"Too bad there isn't any profit in that."

The assembled group had grown silent as they watched the sparring going on between Nicholas and Ali. The Stonebriar Historical Society meetings were usually rather tame affairs compared to the lively debate between the two of them. It was apparent from the exchanged glances Ali saw that she and Nicholas were going to be the topic of conversation in town in the morning.

Ali felt her face flame.

"So what are you going to do?" Nicholas asked, seemingly unconcerned.

"I'll think of something," Ali answered, wanting to end the discussion.

"I'm sure you will."

The meeting continued a while longer with the discussion of new business and then adjourned for cake and coffee.

Ali had planned to stay on after the meeting to talk with the members of the Historical Society to see what she could discover about Nicholas Knight. Alas, Nicholas had stayed on, as she might have guessed he would, considering his sweet tooth, so she left the meeting, knowing little more than she'd known upon arriving.

For the first time, she was tempted to pack it all in and move back to the city. But she knew it would be impossible for her to open a shop there with the high rents. Right now she didn't have a high overhead or a lot invested. Once she sold the tables and chairs, she could combine that money with her profit and open a new shop. As soon as she came up with the right idea.

Besides, she'd almost gotten the feeling Nicholas had actually been enjoying himself, enjoying having an adversary he could fight. Now what did that mean?

She was too much in the dark, she decided, when it came to Nicholas Knight. Tomorrow she was going to Knight's Antiques to have a talk with him. She was going to find out what all this nonsense was about. After all, there was no logical reason that she could think of for him to fight her at every turn.

It was high time they sat down as reasonable adults and discussed their differences. She wondered if Nicholas would be agreeable. Would he keep up that remote distance that protected his feelings?

No matter, she had to try.

NICHOLAS ENTERED the library of the Knight mansion through the open French doors. Still dressed from his visit to the Historical Society meeting, he'd been out tramping through the adjoining property.

Once again he'd thought he'd seen the white specter—*her* ghost, but as always happened, whatever he'd thought he'd seen had disappeared soon after he began investigating it. He'd lost sight of it near the remains of the large stone fireplace.

Maybe he'd only imagined seeing it…maybe he was losing his mind . . . assuming he still had one to lose.

Pouring himself a brandy, he sank onto the sofa. Barely a breeze stirred in the warm, muggy night. The gauzy white curtains at the open doors were still. A storm was brewing and the night waited with a quiet expectancy.

It had been hours since the meeting of the Historical Society had ended. It was long past midnight.

He swirled the brandy in the snifter, the spin of the amber liquid making him dizzy. As dizzy as he'd felt when Ali Charbonneau had walked into the meeting of the Historical Society tonight.

He hadn't been ready for that.

She'd been dressed in a soft pastel print dress. Its long, silky skirt swirled around her coltish legs in an inviting whisper. Her blond hair had been pulled back with pretty combs and hung loose past her shoulders.

She'd looked soft and pretty and the sight of her had made him feel like a real heel.

But Nicholas reminded himself her looks were deceptive. There was nothing soft about Ali Charbonneau. She was as tough as a teamster, holding her ground against him against all odds.

She'd shown him that it would take more than the Health Department and his threats to shut her down for good. Calling in a complaint about her hadn't been the worst thing he'd ever done, but it had been right up there. Especially since his ploy hadn't worked. He might have won this battle, but she was still waging war.

Uttering a curse, he hurled his unwanted brandy at the fireplace. The glass shattered, tinkling in a shower of shards to the floor.

He buried his head in his hands.

A distant roll of thunder reverberated in the room and a flash of brilliant lightning followed not long after. An early splatter of raindrops brought Kashka in to jump onto the sofa beside him. Kashka did not like to be wet.

Licking a few raindrops from her fur, the cat began rubbing against Nicholas and purring. Nicholas picked her up and carried her to the kitchen, where he opened a can of tuna.

"You're spoiled, Kashka. Spoiled rotten—but that seems to be the kind of female I'm attracted to—women who must have their own way at any cost."

Leaving Kashka to her dinner, he climbed the stairs to the second floor. He knew sleep would be impossible in his current state of frustration. In his bedroom, he changed his clothes, pulling on a pair of clean, tattered, paint-stained jeans he didn't even bother to snap.

Going to the south wing, he lit the candles. He liked to paint by candlelight, though he knew it was perverse of him.

Selecting a clean palette and some clean, soft rags, he began rummaging through the drawers of the cabinet where he kept his tubes of paint. Selecting the colors he wanted to work with, he put squiggles of paint onto his palette. Eschewing brushes, he chose a knife. Tonight, as the storm raged both outside and within himself, it suited his mood.

The spring thunderstorm began in earnest, sending small hailstones pinging against the window. Bright splashes of lightning flooded the room as he pushed his dark hair back and drew the knife's edge along the canvas, across the neck of the woman in the portrait. He smiled sardonically, wondering what the rumormongers would say if they could see him.

ALI LAY IN BED, her eyes closed, though she was fully awake. Since the Historical Society meeting Nicholas had refused to leave her thoughts. He frustrated her in every way it was possible for a man to frustrate a woman.

In business he refused to consider her his equal, yet for some reason he considered her a threat. Enough of a threat for him to persist in playing dirty to close her down.

Sexually he played dirty, as well.

There, too, he had to be the one in control, seducing her, then pushing her away when she responded. Instinctively she knew she was some sort of threat to him in that arena, as well. And it had nothing to do with performance. She had every certainty that Nicholas Knight could push buttons she hadn't even known she possessed . . . that he had in fact already done so.

For once she'd like to be the one in control. Just once she'd enjoy teasing and tormenting him sexually, the way he teased and tormented her. At the moment there was only one way she could think of to do just that. Putting his maddening image to good use, she began to indulge in a bit of sensual fantasy. . . .

Nicholas's polished black loafers wore a path in front of the fireplace in the library of the Knight mansion. He stopped pacing abruptly and turned to face her.

He was wearing an appropriately "authoritarian" banker's-blue, pin-striped suit. The look in his dark eyes was his usual one of stern disapproval. "So, once again, young lady, you've disobeyed my wishes."

She sat on the sofa, her hands in her lap, twisting the knit material of her long purple dress in a pretense of demure femininity.

"I'm waiting for you to explain why you disobeyed me," he said with impatience, turning to brace his hand on the mantel, watching her in the mirror above it.

She discarded the demure image, adjusting her response to fit his current mood. "Because I wanted to," she answered, tossing her long blond hair defiantly.

She enjoyed the look of surprise that dawned in his eyes at her display of insubordination. "So then you agree this was no oversight or forgetfulness on your part. You set out to deliberately disobey my wishes?" he asked, his words soft with implied threat.

She pretended a pout. "But you're not being fair...."

He liked that, she could tell; it gave him a surge of power. "Answer the question. You deliberately disobeyed me, didn't you?" His dark eyes held hers captive in the mirror.

"Yes," she said so he could barely hear her and had to look closely at her pouty lips to read them, thus accomplishing her mission of further unnerving him.

"I can't hear you."

"Yes. I deliberately disobeyed your wishes," she agreed, not bothering to hide a self-satisfied smile.

"That doesn't sound like an apology to me," he said, a flicker of uncertainty surfacing in his eyes as he turned to face her, his arms crossed over his chest.

"You're right. It's not an apology. You see, I never had any intention of obeying your wishes. So why don't you discard the verbal reprimand and allow yourself to do what it is you really want to do?" Ali taunted, rising from the sofa to bend across the fringed velvet ottoman.

"What do you think you're doing, young lady?" Nicholas demanded.

Looking over her shoulder, Ali could see he was unable to take his eyes off her angled bottom that she was wiggling with provocative insolence.

"I think you know very well. Don't tell me you haven't been imagining this for a long time. We both know you've wanted to turn me over your knee and spank me since the moment we met." Ali inched up her skirt to reveal the tops of black stockings and purple-ribbon-covered garters.

"Stop." He came toward her then, pulling her to her feet.

"Stop . . . ?"

Tugging her toward the sofa, he sat down, pulling her with him. "I rather prefer the turning you over my knee idea," he explained hoarsely, his hand inching up beneath her long skirt.

"Now wait just a minute! When did he take control?" she muttered, squirming at the delicious, wicked feel of his hand squeezing the bare skin between stocking and satin undergarment.

"The squirming's a nice touch, I like that," she heard Nicholas say with satisfaction. He groaned and she felt the hard evidence of his approval beneath her belly as he slid his hand provocatively over her satin-encased buttocks.

"This was supposed to be a spanking," Ali reminded him. "I don't recall giving you permission to take liberties."

"Right," he said, too agreeably, pushing up her skirt to reveal the erotic temptation of black lace, purple satin and pale skin.

"And now for your punishment, young lady."

"Can the 'young lady' stuff," she said. "I'm a woman."

He brought his hand down, giving her a smart smack. "So you are."

She watched him wait for her reaction and kept her bored pose intact while his hand lingered in a decadent caress.

"You know, I don't think you're being properly contrite," he complained, eyeing her.

"And I don't think the word *proper* enters into this situation in the least."

"I quite agree," Nicholas said. "Let's leave propriety out of this entirely. In fact I think the situation needs a few adjustments." That said, he boldly began making them. First he removed her black kid pumps from her feet. And then he began toying with her satin panties.

"What—what do you think you're doing?" she demanded, forgetting about her pretense of boredom.

"Getting your attention," he assured her. His hand came down again—this time with the mildest of stings, just enough to cause a tingle and a rosy flush.

"Hey!" she objected, squirming in earnest as he became the taunter with a hand that lingered overlong.

"What?" he asked, waiting, arching a dark brow.

"You're taking liberties again...."

"I believe the spanking was your idea, young lady." Now he was baiting her.

"I don't think this is a spanking anymore."

"Really? What is it, then?"

"I meant to punish you. You weren't supposed to have the upper hand again, as you always insist on doing."

His grin was sexy as hell as he looked down at her. "Hey, it's your fantasy...."

He was right.

It was her fantasy. And she wasn't about to continue letting him control it, any more than she was going to allow him to control her in reality. She grinned wickedly and began rewinding the fantasy in her mind. It might take all night, but she'd get it right . . . that is, if Nicholas Knight was up to it.

A naughty, wanton laugh escaped her lips and she began again. . . .

IT WAS THREE in the afternoon, and Ali knew she could no longer put off paying a visit to Knight's Antiques or she'd lose her nerve. She'd promised herself last night she was going to speak one-on-one with Nicholas, and now was as good a time as any.

Slipping her shoulder bag over her arm, she left for his shop. It was time the two of them stopped playing games. They could get around the animosity, the physical attraction, even, if they worked on it together. Surely Nicholas could be made to see the sense of a truce.

The last of the lunch stragglers were leaving Thomure's with homemade pies in hand as she passed by. A few shops farther down she met the police chief.

"Good afternoon, Joe."

"Afternoon," he said, looking up from a license plate that read NV-ME. "You wouldn't be headed over to Knight's Antiques, now, would you?" he asked with a smile.

"Well, yes, as a matter of fact I am, Joe," Ali answered, certain the police chief knew all about last night's quarrel. Thank heavens, he didn't know about her dreams.

"Here tell you two had a little lovers' spat last night over at the Hysterical Society meeting."

"We did not have a . . . we had a disagreement, nothing more," Ali said, flushing.

Joe stepped over a puddle and propped his foot upon the bumper of the expensive foreign car at the curb. "That was quite a frog strangler we had last night."

"Frog strangler?"

"The storm that blew up after midnight. Didn't you hear it?"

"No, I slept right through it. The first hint I had it rained was my soggy newspaper this morning."

"So, you going over to apologize to Nicholas, are you?"

"I don't have anything to apologize for."

"Yeah, well, Jessica doesn't do much apologizing, either. Says it's because she's never wrong."

Ali laughed. "No, it's because you're always the one who's late."

Joe shrugged. "I keep telling her there's no reason to be in such a rush. Hell, I left Saint Louis and a big-city police department because all my friends were dropping dead of stress . . . that and the occasional bullet."

"So Stonebriar's a quiet little town, then, not harboring any murderers . . . ?"

"Murderers?"

"It was just a figure of speech, Joe. Gotta go." Ali was embarrassed by her unsubtle maneuvering.

"Right. You wouldn't happen to know who this car belongs to, now would you?"

Ali shook her head.

The police chief looked at the No Parking sign and back at the car his foot was resting on. "Sure are a lot of city folks that can't read."

"See ya, Joe." Ali waved. A lovers' spat—really! She didn't think she'd ever get used to the small-town gossip mill, especially being grist for it.

Reaching the green-awninged shop a few minutes later, she pushed open the weathered wooden door, which was unlocked despite the Closed sign in the window.

The first thing she noticed about his shop was how clean it was, unlike most antique shops that cultivated dust as part of the ambience. The merchandise was all of high quality. Whatever else one might say about the store's proprietor, he certainly laid valid claim to good taste.

She paused just inside the door at the pine cupboard, taking time to slow her rapidly beating heart and build her courage to approach Nicholas. She picked up a piece of cut-glass stemware from the cupboard display and watched in delight as the afternoon sun streaming in through the front window shot prisms of rainbow color through it.

Glancing around the shop after replacing the stemware, Ali saw that she was the only customer. Perhaps she had come at a fortuitous time to have a discussion with Nicholas. She walked past a display of worn leather suitcases on her way to the back of the shop. She was almost surprised he hadn't put one of those suitcases upon her doorstep as a helpful hint.

"Hello . . . is anyone here?" she called.

No answer.

Perhaps he was on the telephone with a customer, she decided. Giving him a few minutes, she passed the time admiring the exquisite hues of a Tiffany lamp. After a few minutes it occurred to her that she wasn't hearing any conversation.

She ventured into the open doorway.

"Hello . . . Nicholas?"

He wasn't there. She could come back later, but her courage might desert her. She could just stay and wait for him to return, and he could accuse her of snooping. Wouldn't he love that after her accusations about Kashka!

Still, temptation coaxed her into the office. Curiosity kept her there long past what was prudent.

The walls of what was clearly his office were painted a glossy deep green, but they were empty of any decoration. The room itself was windowless, devoid of any view of the outside world.

She glanced around. Nowhere did she see a framed photograph of family member, friend or lover. The room announced that its occupant wanted no personal ties.

Even the oak file cabinets along one wall were plantless. It was a small thing, but telling.

A large rolltop desk stood against the back wall. The local paper sat on top, still rolled up.

Intrigued, she went to the desk for a quick look around. It was very neat, with a desk phone set on the right side and a small beige lamp on the other side. In the middle a dragon paperweight rested on a pile of neatly stacked invoices. A fat fountain pen, black with gold trim, lay open beside them.

She wondered what Nicholas's handwriting looked like. Her own, she knew, reflected her enthusiastic personality, sprawling willy-nilly across the paper.

A notepad near the phone provided her with an answer. He'd doodled her name on the pad in a bold but closed script—and then crossed it out with strong strokes.

Had she been getting to him? Had he been angry to be daydreaming about her? Or did it mean something more ominous? No. She was letting her imagination run away again.

A parking ticket in one of the cubbyholes of the desk caught her eye. She smiled, recalling Joe Allen's comment. Evidently it wasn't only city folk who didn't know how to read. She leaned closer to make out the ticket's faint printing.

The sudden ringing of the telephone startled her into jumping back like someone caught with her hand in the till. Her hand flew to her chest and felt her heart beating double time. She took a deep breath to calm herself.

The phone kept ringing until the answering machine took over.

After the brief message that the caller had reached Knight's Antiques and three short beeps, a woman's petulant voice came over the line.

"Hello, Nicholas . . . it's Heather."

Heather?

"You haven't called me. . . . I thought we had such fun at Coral Court. . . ."

Coral Court?

"I've been wanting to thank you personally for the lovely gown you sent to replace the one you ripped."

Ripped?

"I've bought you a present from Victoria's Secret . . . call me."

The hussy.

"Me-oow." Kashka's commentary was apt; she jumped onto the desk, startling Ali once again. Turning, Ali fully expected to see Nicholas's disapproving scowl.

But the shop was still empty. Kashka must have been asleep in one of the baskets scattered throughout the shop. The ringing telephone had probably awakened her. How, she wondered, as she watched Kashka sit licking her paw with lazy interest, had Heather's gown gotten ripped?

While Ali tormented herself with images, Kashka's long black tail dropped across the center drawer of the desk.

Would she dare open it?

It would be a clear invasion of privacy. If she left now, she could salve her conscience by the fact that everything she'd seen had been technically on public view, even if it was in his private office.

She glanced at her watch and wondered how much longer Nicholas might stay away. Perhaps he'd run over to Thomure's for some take-out food. Taking a cursory glance around the still empty shop, Ali gave in to curiosity and slipped open the center drawer of the desk. Inside was a silver letter opener with a K monogram on it, a scattering of stamps and some blank postcards with a picture of Knight's Antiques for the out-of-town tourists to Stonebriar.

Emboldened, she tried another drawer, to find only a cache of art magazines. Feeling guilty, she ceased her furtive search and turned to go. In her haste she knocked the newspaper from its rather precarious perch on the top of the desk.

Ali bent to retrieve the newspaper from where it had rolled, near the tall file, and made a discovery.

Someone had shoved a painting behind the file.

Her curiosity renewed, Ali tugged at the painting until it came free. Alarm swept over her when she got a look at the painting.

It was a portrait—her likeness.

And it had been viciously slashed.

7

ALI STOOD MOTIONLESS, staring at her disturbing discovery. The vandalized painting hinted at a darkness in Stonebriar she hadn't wanted to believe existed. Was she placing herself in danger by disregarding the cryptic remarks of some of the townspeople?

Had she been mistaken about Nicholas's cool hostility? Was he mad? Surely not. She couldn't be attracted to a madman.

Willing her leaden limbs to move, she replaced the slashed painting in its hiding place, hoping her snooping wouldn't be uncovered. Her mind racing with a jumble of thoughts and emotions, she hurried from the empty shop before she could be discovered.

She needed time to think.

Maybe leaving Stonebriar was the right thing to do, after all.

A LONG NIGHT'S SLEEP and hours of early-morning rumination over a pot of tea helped Ali to make up her mind. She decided she would stay in Stonebriar and open a new shop.

After she'd considered Nicholas's actions in a calmer emotional state, she had come to the conclusion that they were defensive rather than offensive tactics. And while the slashed painting continued to alarm her, her alarm was tempered by the loneliness the office in his antique shop demonstrated. The slashed painting could reflect emotional frustration.

The only person who seemed to have a relationship with Nicholas with any degree of closeness was Jessica. Somehow Ali knew instinctively Heather was more dalliance than anything, their intimacy only physical.

Maybe she was kidding herself, but she felt Nicholas needed her. Needed her so badly that it frightened him—into pushing her away. They seemed on some unspoken level to know each other...match each other.

The third time had to be a charm, as the saying went. She couldn't keep changing shops at this dizzying pace. This had to be the one.

She had only this morning gotten the idea for the kind of shop that would thwart Nicholas, as well as be something she truly wanted to run. The idea had come to her while thinking about Nicholas's actions.

He probably would not be pleased to know he was the one who had actually inspired her plan. The suggestion he'd made at the meeting of the Historical Society that she open a dressmaking shop had been purposefully chauvinistic and condescending.

She'd give him a dressmaking shop.

He wanted her to do something feminine that didn't compete with his shop or any of the others, did he? Well, the shop she was going to open would set Nicholas Knight upon his ear.

Recalling the trunk full of exquisite lingerie she'd inherited from her grandmother, she'd decided to open a quality lingerie shop. She wouldn't even have to change the decor of the tearoom; it already had the right ambience. All she needed to do was sell the tables and chairs and replace them with display pieces for the lingerie. Her only expense would be her inventory.

She smiled, thinking of the message she'd overheard on Nicholas's answering machine when she'd been snooping in his office. Perhaps he'd even send a little business to her by way of Heather . . . what with all the bodice ripping he evidently indulged in.

Ali poured herself another cup of tea and walked around the tearoom, considering how she wanted to set up the lingerie shop, what kind of display pieces she wanted to use. She'd continue to keep the antique hotel register on a stand by the door, of course. It had been her good-luck charm from the beginning, as well as a valuable source for mailing announcements to customers. The antique shop and tearoom had done well enough, despite Nicholas's eventual success in closing them.

She went to the large display window in the front of the store where Kashka was dozing. Looking out, she quickly jumped back. Nicholas was heading toward her shop with a picnic hamper in his hand.

What was he up to now?

She was still taking deep breaths when he opened the door and came inside.

"Kashka is in the window," she said with a nod, trying not to notice the big basket.

"I'm not here for Kashka. I've given up on her coming here."

"Then why are you here?"

"I thought we could have a picnic lunch and talk."

"We're on speaking terms?"

"I don't know. Are we?" he asked, waiting with quiet intensity.

He'd come to her once before to make amends, failing miserably. Maybe he was making another effort. If he was offering a truce, she would be foolish to turn him down.

"What do you want to talk about?"

"Your plans."

"Oh, no, I'm not telling you my plans so you can sabotage me once again."

"I only want to talk."

She stared at him. "Don't you think you did enough talking last night at the meeting?"

He didn't answer, just stood there, returning her stare.

Suddenly her jeans felt too tight, her cropped cotton sweater seemed too skimpy. She tugged nervously at her ponytail.

He stood there, cool and calm in his fresh white shirt, jeans and sockless loafers. He smelled fresh from a shower while she could feel herself perspiring, growing moist and clammy. He made her so uneasy she could scream. Perhaps, considering the painting she'd discovered, she should scream.

She agreed to the picnic.

Twenty minutes later she found herself sitting beside him on a quilt on the bank of the river, eating the lunch he'd had Thomure's prepare.

By unspoken agreement they remained silent as they ate, enjoying the glorious afternoon. The leafy tree above cast dappled sunlight over them. Nearby a squirrel sat on its haunches, nibbling at something in its tiny paws.

Butterflies flitted here and there with the attention span of a toddler. The drone of a pair of honeybees added to the seductive lull of the warm afternoon, inviting them to linger over the simple lunch of cheese, bread and fruit.

"That about does it for the tasty morsels," Ali said when they finished a small apple dessert.

"I wouldn't know about that," Nicholas replied, leisurely rolling the sleeves of his white shirt to his elbows.

She admired his muscled strength. Was he dangerous? Had she been foolish to come with him?

Nicholas didn't say any more. Instead he poured the last of the wine into the glasses. He handed her one of them and clinked his against hers. "To acceptance," he toasted.

"Acceptance of what?" she asked, looking at him with wary eyes and thinking twice about drinking any more of the wine. She set down her glass on the quilt, "accidentally" tipping it over so that it spilled.

"The inevitable," he answered, reaching for some paper napkins to soak up the spilled wine. He disposed of the napkins in the picnic basket, then moved closer.

"What . . . what's inevitable?" she asked, hearing her voice crack a little.

"The fact that you won't leave here."

"What?" *He was dangerous!*

"You've convinced me you won't leave Stonebriar until you're ready," he said with a shrug, lying back on the quilt.

Ali expelled a shaky breath. She really was going to have to do something about her wild imagination.

"Why are you so adamant about my leaving Stonebriar?" she asked, lying back in her turn and looking at the clear blue sky above. The few clouds were puffy and friendly, reminding her of the childhood game of making out shapes. She saw a heart, struck by Cupid's arrow.

"Why are you so adamant about staying? This isn't your life. Your business is only a temporary fling to you. It's something to do until you settle into the life your parents groomed you for. Soon you'll grow bored and move on."

"That's not it. You just don't like me. You haven't liked me since the day we met. I think it's because you're a . . ."

"A chauvinist?"

"A knight in heavy armor to protect your heart."

He levered his body toward her. Slowly running his thumb back and forth across her bottom lip in a teasing fashion, he disagreed. "I like you."

Lowering his head, he brushed her lips with his. He began taking little eating kisses, stealing her breath. "We both know there's this attraction between us," he whispered hoarsely between kisses.

"You feel it, you know you do. Don't lie to yourself—or to me."

"Yes, I feel it," she admitted as his hand wrapped around the curve of her waist, pulling her to him. Then he deepened his kiss—a kiss that was more drugging than the wine they'd shared earlier.

Ali felt shamelessly wanton, responding to his whispered encouragement.

His hand slipped beneath her cropped sweater, cupping her soft satin bra. He squeezed her gently, while his tongue slipped past the barrier of her teeth to plunder the sweetness beyond.

Ali couldn't think, could see nothing; everything receded but the delicious, wicked feelings Nicholas continued to elicit from her wildly excited body.

A body that was more than willing to play any game he chose.

By any rules.

His rules.

His long fingers pushed up her bra and sweater, freeing tender skin to the warm kiss of the afternoon sun, the caress of a gentle breeze.

Her hands were in his dark hair, urging his ardent caress, demanding the laving, sucking that spiraled white-hot streamers of desire through her veins to pool in a heavy ache at her center.

His hand cupped the juncture of her jeans-clad thighs, rubbing, teasing until she moved. He responded by slowly lowering the zipper of her jeans and bending his head to bite gently at the exposed skin above her bikini panties in the V of the opened zipper.

Ali squirmed beneath his touch, not thinking, only giving herself up to the sensations he orchestrated with his oh, so talented hands and mouth. When his fingers slipped beneath the elastic of her panties, she was moist and ready. She arched toward him.

"Just a minute, hold on," he said, stopping, turning away.

Ali was pleased that *he*'d remembered protection, was man enough to use it.

"Don't you have something to tell me?" Nicholas's words broke the sensual spell.

Tell him? He wanted to talk? *Now?*

"Look at me," he demanded.

She blinked open her eyes, but it was hard to see at first in the bright sunlight.

She'd expected to see him—naked and proud.

But when she finally focused to the light, he wasn't naked. He was proud, tough, and completely dressed.

There was censure in his eyes as he studied her. Finally he spoke. "What is your game exactly? How far are you willing to go to get what you want? Are you a reporter? Is that why you're really here, snooping around to get a story?"

"I don't know what you're talking about," Ali declared, not fathoming where he was going with his accusations or why.

"Really? I suppose, then, this isn't your watch, either?" he asked; she saw the delicate watch her parents had given her dangling from his forefinger.

"Where did you . . . ?"

She felt the blood drain from her face as she remembered where she might have lost it, remembered checking the time.

"I found it in my shop."

Ali swallowed dryly, trying to look innocent. "I didn't know I'd lost it. I hadn't missed it yet. The catch doesn't always work and I've been meaning to get it repaired," she lied. "I stopped at your shop yesterday, but you weren't in."

"I see. . . ."

"Where did you find it exactly?"

"In my office."

"Well, as I said, I was looking for you. . . ."

"Yes, you said so."

Oh, no. Had he found it behind the file cabinet by the slashed painting? Had her watch come loose when she'd shoved the painting back into its hiding place? What would he do if he knew she knew about the painting?

"You were snooping, weren't you? You went to the shop when it was closed— I leave it unlocked when I'm not going to be gone long. I figure most people respect a Closed sign in the window. Besides, I can see my place from Thomure's."

"You were at Thomure's?"

He nodded.

"Not hard to figure. I usually go over for a bit of coffee and pie that time of day. But then you'd know that, if you were watching for your opportunity."

"I wasn't watching you . . . I'm not a reporter. I'm exactly what I say I am."

"I don't know whether to believe you or not. I do know I want you to leave Stonebriar. Some things you don't put together because the combination is dangerous. You and I are—not a good idea."

"I . . . you . . . you and I . . ." Ali was so angry she couldn't speak. He'd been in control the whole time he'd played at seducing her. It was only she who'd lost control at his touch.

He was a monster.

IT TOOK SOME DOING, but Ali was open for business in a few short weeks. Attic Treasures was the name she'd chosen for her lingerie shop. While Jessica had been out of town visiting a friend, she had given Ali her permission by phone and had even sent a new sign for the shop as a surprise.

Ali looked at her watch . . . and thought of Nicholas. They hadn't spoken since the day of the picnic.

Kashka was another story.

She wandered by every day and lingered until she got her saucer of milk. At the moment she sat contentedly atop the cash register, her long tail swinging back and forth like a pendulum. A noise at the door caught her attention and Ali, too, looked expectantly at the door.

The door opened and Kashka jumped down to greet her master, meowing and twining herself between his feet.

Nicholas's gaze swept over the profusion of pastel and brightly hued lingerie displayed on old-fashioned dressing screens; a scattering of teddy bears was seated on assorted odd chairs.

"*This* is what you think people have in their attics?" he asked, referring to the name of her shop.

"No. I'm sure you have bats in yours."

"Probably," he said with a shrug. "And an old fielder's mitt, too," he added, deliberately misunderstanding to annoy her. "That's what most people have in their attics—old things."

"You mean like skeletons?" she asked to bait him.

"No, those go in closets...."

He was so infuriatingly smug. "Just go away. There's no way you're going to close me down again."

"I'm not here to close you down, though closing down this bordello would be an easy enough... eh... proposition."

"This is *not* a bordello."

"Right."

"Why are you here?"

"It isn't my idea, believe me. Jessica sent me."

"Jessica?"

"I spoke with her last night when she returned from her trip. She'll be by to see your new shop soon, but she sent me over to have a look at the roof, said you'd told her you thought you'd noticed a small leak."

"Oh."

"So if you'll point me to where the leak is, I'll have a look and be gone."

At that moment the shop door opened and two women came inside.

"The leak is right over the tub in the bathroom," Ali informed Nicholas, then went to wait on the two women.

"May I help you?"

The two looked up from the teddy bear in a pink camisole they were admiring.

"Why, hello, it's Agnes and Edith, isn't it?" Ali said, recognizing the women to whom she'd sold the camel-back trunk with the romantic story that had so angered Nicholas.

"Why, yes," the two women agreed, smiling their delight at being recognized. "But dear, isn't that Nicholas Knight who owns Knight's Antiques you just allowed upstairs?"

"Yes...."

"Are you sure that's wise?" Edith asked. "I overheard some locals saying he'd murdered someone years ago and gotten away with it. You really can't be too careful these days, you know."

"That's just idle, small-town gossip. I'm sure Nicholas hasn't murdered anyone. He's not very friendly, but that doesn't mean he's dangerous, ladies."

"Well, you be careful," they chorused.

"I promise," Ali agreed. "I'm so pleased you've come back to visit my shop."

"We received your lovely notice in the mail about the tearoom replacing the antique shop, but we didn't get a chance to come out," Agnes said.

"We were just planning to visit when we got your new notice that you'd changed your shop again," Edith added.

"It's a long story," Ali told them at their look of confusion. "But I think I've settled on the right kind of store for me now. Why don't you two ladies take your time browsing? If you'll excuse me for a moment, I need to run upstairs and check on something."

Nicholas had been up there plenty long enough to have checked to see the leak in her bathroom ceiling. What was he doing?

Upstairs, Ali expected to find Nicholas looking through her things. But while Kashka was asleep on her bed, Nicholas appeared to have vanished. Then she noticed the open window and decided he'd climbed out onto the roof. His footsteps overhead a few moments later confirmed her suspicion. Leaving him to his inspection, Ali hurried back downstairs to her customers.

"How are you doing, ladies? Have you found anything you like?"

"Yes, this bear," Edith said, lifting the one with the pink camisole that had first caught her eye.

"But it isn't for—" Ali caught herself. There wasn't any reason she couldn't sell the bears as well as the lingerie, or even the old-fashioned dressing screens, should a customer desire to purchase one. "If you want the bear, it's yours. I'll remove the camisole and . . ."

"Oh, no, dear. I want the bear to wear it. I have a collection of bears—all of them dressed in different fashion. I want to buy both the bear and the camisole."

Ali rang up the sale and chatted with the two women while she wrapped the bear.

"My niece, Melissa, would love this shop, don't you think, Agnes?" Edith asked her friend.

Edith nodded. "But right now I'm starving. We need to hurry if we're going to get to Thomure's before they run out of the taco salad."

"I'll look forward to meeting Melissa," Ali said, handing Edith the bear.

As the two ladies exited, Billy Lawrence entered. "Where are the models?" he asked, surveying the shop with lascivious relish. "I hope they've just taken a lunch break."

"Where's Caroline?" Ali asked in return, hoping she had only been delayed at another shop.

"What, you're not happy to see just me?"

"What are you doing here, Billy?"

"I got your invitation," he said, pulling the notice announcing the opening of Attic Treasures from the back pocket of his khaki pants. "I thought I'd come out here and browse through your lingerie." The way he said it made it sound personal . . . made her skin crawl.

"I sent that to Caroline, not you."

"I know, I lifted it."

"Go home, Billy."

"Now is that any way to treat a paying customer?" he demanded, making no move to leave.

"You're here to buy something?" Ali asked, looking at him doubtfully. Billy never had any money on him. He was a mooch of the first order.

"Sure. I can buy something. I can do that. I could get Caroline a . . . little surprise, I suppose."

"Okay, what would you like?"

With a dirty grin he asked, "You got any of those panties that—?"

"No."

"What kind of place is this?"

Ali folded her arms in front of her. "It's a quality lingerie shop. Every item in the shop is not only beautiful, it's tasteful, as well. I'm quite sure there's nothing here you'd like."

"I don't know," Billy said, clearly refusing to take her hint. "Why don't you show me what you've got and let me be the judge of what I might like?" His eyes roved over her. "Why don't you show me what you look like in this?" He lifted a rich gold lace bra from one of the old-fashioned dressing screens with one finger.

"Forget it, Billy."

"No? Then how about this?" he suggested, picking up the matching scalloped lace bikini panties.

"Billy..."

"Don't give me that 'Billy' stuff. We both know it's all available when the right offer is made."

"I don't know what you're talking about, Billy. And I don't care. I want you to leave."

Billy moved closer. She almost suffocated on his expensive designer cologne. "Oh, I think you know what I'm talking about, all right," he said, swinging the lace bikini panties back and forth on his finger. "It's real simple. You be nice to me, *real nice,* and I could break my engagement for you."

"And I'll break your neck for you."

Billy spun around at the sound of a man's deep voice behind him. "Where the hell did you come from?" he demanded.

Nicholas shrugged. His loafers and shirt were up in Ali's room. He'd taken them off when he'd gone out to nail down a loose shingle. His jeans were comfortably unsnapped. He knew *exactly* how it looked when he said, "Upstairs."

Billy looked from Nicholas to Ali, a sneer lacing his words. "So it's like that, is it?"

"No," Ali quickly objected.

"Yes."

"Were the two of you already involved when you were playing footsie with me beneath the table the day we all had lunch together, Ali?" Billy accused her sanctimoniously.

"I never . . ."

"That was me, you idiot . . . showing you what a jerk you are," Nicholas said.

So that was where Billy had gotten the idea she'd been encouraging him. Had Nicholas really played footsie with Billy? She wouldn't have believed Nicholas had that much sense of humor—or that he had a sense of humor at all.

"I believe you were leaving," Nicholas prompted Billy.

"Not before I make my purchase."

"I believe Ali has already established that what you want isn't for sale."

"Nicholas!" Ali knew her face was crimson.

"Why, I oughta . . ." Billy was plainly furious, his fists clenched at his sides.

"No, that wouldn't be wise. It would be wise for you to leave before I really get angry. You don't want to be around when I'm really angry—ask around town."

"You're crazy!" Billy accused, backing out of the shop.

"That's what they say," Nicholas said with a shrug.

"You let him believe . . ." Ali said when Nicholas turned back to her.

"Billy doesn't understand subtleties. Maybe now he'll leave you alone."

"I want you to leave."

"Sure, but first I have to retrieve my shirt and shoes."

"I'll get them. Wait here."

As he waited he wondered what it was that came over him whenever another man laid claim to Ali. He didn't wonder long. He knew. Jealousy. Not a pretty emotion and certainly not a safe one. If he were smart he'd stay the hell away from Ali Charbonneau. Surely in all this time he'd learned that much about a woman like her? He couldn't allow the past to repeat itself.

He had to stop and think about what he was doing.

No. He had to stop, period.

Ali came back a few minutes later with his shirt and shoes to find him holding up a burgundy bodysuit made of lace interspersed with soft, stretch panne velvet.

"What are you doing?"

"Shopping."

"For Heather?" The words, fueled by jealousy, were out before she knew it. She wanted to bite her tongue.

"Who?"

"Nothing."

"I believe you said Heather."

"No, I didn't. Why would I say Heather?"

"Ali . . ."

"What?"

"I'll take it," he said, tossing her the burgundy body-suit.

She wrote up the sale, packaged the suit and watched him leave, the whole while consumed with jealousy. He'd bought Heather a gift. An intimate gift.

Tonight she wouldn't lie awake entertaining herself with a fantasy. No, tonight she'd lie awake torturing herself with one . . . one in which Heather wore burgundy lingerie and Nicholas ripped it from her perfect body.

8

"THE SHOP IS LOVELY, Ali," Jessica said after a leisurely perusal. "But so were the antique shop . . . and the tearoom." There was an unasked question in her comment.

"I think this is the one that will really stick," Ali answered. "You know it's funny, Jessica. You can never predict what will work in a business. The lingerie is selling really well, but what surprises me is that I'm selling almost as many of the painted chairs the bears sit on, the old-fashioned dressing screens and even the bears themselves."

"That doesn't surprise me." Jessica slipped on her glasses and studied the detailing on a silk robe. "The shop is so upbeat, fanciful and pretty, people naturally want to take a little of that home with them." Hanging up the robe, she turned to Ali. "Oh, I meant to ask. Did Nicholas come by and check on the leak in the roof you found?"

"Yes. And fixed it."

"Good. Now," Jessica said, slipping her arm through Ali's, "let's see if we can't find something here among your lovely things to cure Joe of his tardiness. What do you recommend?"

"Jessica!"

"Well, I may not be twenty, dear, but I'm hardly dead."

Ali laughed at Jessica's exaggerated wink and set about helping her make a selection from the more provocative items she stocked.

When they were through, Jessica took the items behind one of the dressing screens to try them on.

Ali fiddled with putting a satin bed jacket on one of the bears while she worked up the courage to question Jessica about her godson. Now was the perfect time; she wouldn't have to look Jessica in the eye. She felt foolish enough, as it was.

But she needed to know about the slashed painting she'd found behind the file cabinet in Nicholas's office. What did it mean? Was the man she was half in love with, despite the mixed signals he kept sending her, a complex, emotionally closed man or was he dangerous . . . ?

She took a deep breath.

Jessica began for her. "So how are you and my godson getting along?" she asked, laying her suit jacket over the top of the dressing screen.

"I'm not sure."

"You're not sure?"

"Nicholas is . . . well, you know, difficult."

"Yes, I know."

"I need to talk to you about something, Jessica. I hope you won't think I'm being . . ."

"What is it, dear?" Jessica's suit skirt followed her jacket to the top of the dressing screen.

"The other day I went to Nicholas's shop. I wanted to talk with him, but he wasn't there. When he didn't come after a while, I decided to look around."

"He has some nice things, doesn't he? I'm especially partial to the Tiffany lamp. Does he still have it?"

"Yes. Yes, it's very pretty." Ali took another deep breath; this was the part where she had to admit she had been snooping in Nicholas's office. "Jessica . . ."

"Yes. Oh, my goodness! How am I ever supposed to get this thing snapped?"

Ali chuckled when she heard Jessica swear and then say, "There, I got it. I guess I'm more limber than I thought. Hmm . . . yes, I think this little number is just the thing for Joe."

Her head popped around the corner of the dressing screen. "What was it you were asking me, dear?"

"I was about to tell you that while I was in Nicholas's shop I discovered something rather disquieting I wanted to ask you about."

"What's that?" Jessica asked, returning to her task.

"Ah, I was in Nicholas's office. . . ." A sudden inspiration struck Ali. "The phone had rung, and not knowing Nicholas had an answering machine, I'd gone into his office to answer it. While I was there, something odd caught my eye and being the curious sort, I'm afraid I gave in to temptation and went to investigate."

"What was it you saw?" Jessica asked, tossing the teddy she'd just removed over the dressing screen and selecting something else to try.

"When I went to see what was sticking out from behind one of the tall file cabinets, I discovered it was a framed painting."

"Did you say a *painting?*"

"Yes."

"I do hope Nicholas has taken my advice and begun his painting again. But why was he hiding the painting behind a file cabinet?"

"I think he hid it there because he didn't want anyone to see it."

"I don't know why he can't believe he's a marvelous painter. Just because his first gallery showing was unfortunate is no reason for him to dwell on the criticism of his work. There was a reason then...." Jessica's voice faded as she reached for her suit to begin getting dressed again.

"I don't think he'd put the painting there because he was doubting its quality," Ali said.

"Then why?"

"The painting was badly damaged. It had been viciously slashed."

"Oh, no!"

"Yes. And Jessica . . . the painting was my likeness."

"Oh, dear."

Jessica came around the dressing screen, dressed in her suit again. Her beringed hand massaged her throat. Sighing, she picked up the black teddy she'd selected and handed it to Ali. "Here, wrap this for me, dear, and then we'll go upstairs and talk. It's almost closing time, anyway."

When Ali had completed the sale and wrapped the garment, she turned the sign in the window to Closed and they went upstairs.

Jessica took the white wicker rocker while Ali sat across from her on the bed.

"This painting you saw," Jessica began. "Was it a portrait?"

Ali nodded.

"What was the girl in the portrait wearing?"

"I don't remember . . . something green, I think. Yes, it was a green velvet dress."

Jessica nodded, as if she'd expected the answer. "That wasn't you in the painting, dear. I know it must have been alarming to find a painting slashed like that—"

"I don't understand. Who is the woman?"

A faraway look came into Jessica's eyes, and she rocked slowly back and forth a few moments before answering. "The painting was of Camilla Hawthorne."

"I don't understand."

"I know, dear. I guess I should have told you about Camilla sooner, but I didn't want to resurrect the past. As it is, Nicholas lives in it too much. The portrait, you see, was painted before the terrible fire."

"Is that what—?"

"Yes. A fire destroyed the Hawthorne mansion, burning it to the ground one night. Hawthorne House's only marker is the crumbling foundation that remains next door to the Knight mansion. I keep telling Nicholas he should have the ruins razed since he owns the property, but he won't hear of it. He keeps them there as some sort of horrible monument. Camilla, of course, lived there."

"Then the painting is fifteen years old."

Jessica nodded. "You favor Camilla. It's uncanny how much. You gave us a start when we first saw you. She had the same blond hair, the same brown eyes. She was tall and slender like you, as well.

"She commissioned Nicholas to paint the portrait to hang over the fireplace. I'd always assumed the painting perished in the fire."

Ali got up and walked over to the window to look outside. She didn't know how to ask Jessica the next question. Finally she just asked it without preamble. "Was there some sort of scandal connected with the fire? Is that what everyone keeps dropping me cryptic hints about? There's one shopkeeper who has even gone so far as to accuse Nicholas of being a murderer. Surely that can't be true."

Jessica twisted one of the rings on her finger. "So then you've heard all the rumors. I should have guessed you might with Stonebriar being such a small town. I thought everything had died down, it all happened fifteen years ago. But I guess scandals have a life of their own, feeding on innuendo and half truths."

"Will you tell me what really happened?" Ali asked expectantly, returning from the window to sit on the bed.

Jessica shook her head, a sad look crossing her face. "No one is entirely sure. But I can tell you what's at the bottom of the rumors. The fire happened at three o'clock in the morning. It was out of control before anyone reported it to the fire department. Camilla Hawthorne died in the fire."

"How terrible."

"I know. Camilla lived alone in the house. Her mother and father were killed in a boating accident when she was eighteen, right after her father had bankrupted them with a bad investment."

"That's certainly tragic . . . but not scandalous," Ali observed.

"There were rumors that Camilla had seduced a married man. She was a wild one, always had to have her way. After her father's death she got worse. It was as if she was bent on a path of self-destruction. When Nicholas's father's body was found in the ashes of Hawthorne House, along with Camilla's, it was clear who the married man she was having an affair with was. The fact that he was nearly twice her age made it all the more damning. Scandals are started with much less fuel than that, my dear."

"But that still doesn't explain the whispers about Nicholas being a murderer. . . ." Ali couldn't refrain from wondering aloud.

Jessica stopped rocking and looked directly at Ali.

"That, dear, is where speculation takes over from fact. To begin with, it was a fact that there was a fire late in the night and that Nicholas's father and Camilla Hawthorne were together at Hawthorne House at three in the morning, but after that point no one knows what really happened—except the two of them. And, of course, they aren't here to tell anyone. Every gossip in town was ready with a theory of his or her own, but there seem to be two that time has settled on.

"One is that Nicholas's father set the fire in a murder-suicide for some unknown reason. Maybe Camilla wanted to break it off. A grown man can act more adolescent than a teenager when in the throes of a full-blown love affair. I'm sure the fact that Nicholas's grandfather committed suicide in the Knight mansion only whipped up such speculation."

"And the other theory?" Ali prompted, sensing that it held the answer she was seeking.

"That Nicholas killed them both because he loved his mother so, and then set the fire. Nicholas's mother died not long after of a sudden illness—a congestion, caught from being out in the rain, walking the ruins."

Ali sat quiet for a moment, reeling at the tragedy of Nicholas's life. "What do you think happened that night?" she finally asked.

"I don't know," Jessica said, her voice a murmur. "I've always thought whatever happened was a terrible accident."

"Was Nicholas charged for murder?"

"No, there wasn't evidence to charge him, though that didn't stop the rumors to this day, as you know. Some people will always think he set the fire. He's been punished ever since.

"Everything Nicholas had worked so hard for, all his dreams went up in flames that night. A year's work of paintings he was readying for his first gallery showing were at the Hawthorne House. Camilla was handling the framing for Nicholas. The gallery owner was a friend of hers. Those paintings were destroyed in the fire."

"But I thought you said Nicholas had had a gallery showing, that it hadn't gone well."

"Oh, he did—a year later," Jessica agreed, staring into space. "His new paintings, however, were savaged by the critics. He didn't sell a single painting, and as far as I know, he hasn't painted since, though I keep encouraging him to try."

"It's so sad."

"That it is, dear. That it is."

"At least I'm relieved to find out that the painting wasn't of me," Ali said softly, "though I have to admit the fact that it was slashed is still very disturbing." A shiver shook her. "The emotion behind that act was potent, frightening in its intensity."

Jessica nodded. "I agree. I'm sure finding the painting gave you a fright. But perhaps the slashing was an outpouring of grief by Nicholas over his father's death, along with the scandal of it, not madness."

Ali considered Jessica's premise. "At least now know why Nicholas hates me...."

"I'm sure he doesn't hate you, dear." Jessica reached to pat Ali's hand reassuringly. "In fact, you're the first person he's shown any response to in the fifteen years since the fire."

Ali didn't have the heart to tell Jessica that the only interest Nicholas had in her was in closing her down—putting her out of business, so she'd have to leave Stonebriar. But now that she knew more about his background, Ali could be more understanding of the demons that drove him.

Her life, in contrast, had been a charmed existence.

"Well, I'll be going now, dear," Jessica said, getting up from the white rocker. "You let me know if you have any trouble with the roof leaking. I'm not sure how handy Nicholas is when it comes to making home repairs. From the state of the Knight mansion, I'd say not very."

"Here, don't forget your package," Ali said, handing Jessica the teddy she'd wrapped for her earlier in her signature apricot and violet print bag, tied with mint-green ribbon.

Jessica took the package and smiled. "Thanks. Joe doesn't know it, but he's about to find out how dangerous a woman with a plan can be."

AFTER JESSICA LEFT, Ali fixed a microwave dinner and settled in to relax with a good book. An hour later she gave up when she realized she had finished the dinner a half hour ago and had been reading the same two pages over and over ever since. Her mind kept straying from the story on the page to the tale Jessica had told her.

Nicholas's past fascinated her, and the Knight mansion was drawing her like a magnet.

Giving in to the inevitable, she closed the book. After tossing the remains of the dinner into the trash, she threw a chambray shirt over her T-shirt and walking shorts and headed out.

It was dusk, and twinkling lights were beginning to show on the highway in the distance as cars wound their way home in streamers of red and white light. Birds quieted, settling into treetops, and the wind carried up the scent of the night from the river. Drawn on by the promise of the night, she found herself at the big, black iron fence surrounding Nicholas's home. The Knight mansion loomed cold and foreboding, shrouded in darkness. No familiar light shone in the south wing.

Nicholas must have gone out for the evening.

A pang of jealousy hit her as she pictured Heather. Had he gone to her? In her mind's eye she could still see the burgundy silk slipping through his long fingers.

She knew his touch—knew what those artist's fingers could do.

A sudden blur to her right stopped her in mid muse and she froze. What had she seen?

If she turned to look more closely, would it disappear once more? She should just leave well enough alone. But since she'd never been tempted to try leaving well enough alone, curiosity won out once again. She turned.

No, she hadn't imagined it.

It was still there, whatever it was. It appeared to be a woman in white. No, the figure was translucent. Could it really be a . . . a ghost?

She felt a shiver of fear followed by a prickle of awed fascination. Was she seeing Camilla Hawthorne's ghost—could that be possible? The figure was once again inside the ruins of Hawthorne House.

Was Camilla...er...Camilla's ghost trying to tell her something? She shook her head, annoyed with herself. She was trying to use logic to make sense of a completely ridiculous fancy.

There were no ghosts.

Well, she'd never seen one.

Not until now, anyway. Maybe if she moved closer, she would come up with a logical explanation, one that didn't involve ghosts.

It could be nothing more than a trick of the moonlight glancing off a shred of mist from the river. From this distance it could be anything.

Or it could really be a ghost. Did she really want to know?

Yes.

Taking several deep breaths, she ventured into the ill-kept property, making her way gingerly across the deep, wide expanse of overgrown lawn. Mindful of the fall she'd taken when she'd tried to run from Nicholas, she was careful to watch where she placed her feet.

As she drew closer, the white specter moved as well until it stood near the remains of the fireplace.

Ali was moving toward the fireplace when she caught sight of a figure approaching from the direction of the Knight mansion. Reacting instinctively, she dropped to the ground to avoid being silhouetted in the moonlight. She caught the faint scent of flowers and looked down to see she was crouching near a patch of yellow and purple crocuses among a scattering of half-sprouted green stems, harbingers of what would soon be a field of yellow daffodils.

As she watched, concealed by the darkness, the ghost faded until it had disappeared altogether, exactly upon the man's arrival. In the moonlight she could see it was a disheveled Nicholas. His dark stubble made him look dangerous, a look further enhanced by his wildly mussed hair and wrinkled clothing.

Was this the monster he'd warned her of?

If it was, it was a man at war with himself. For while his appearance was disturbing, his face reflected the ravages of a tormented soul.

The wail of his voice was devoid of hope as he slumped to his knees, his words, "Why am I cursed...why...why...?" full of angry frustration, seeming stubbornly to accept, yet deny his fate.

It was painful for Ali to watch.

She wanted to go to him, to comfort him. To bring him out of the dark and into the light.

But now was not the time.

He would not thank her for invading his vulnerable privacy. Seeing him out of control had not repelled her, but touched her deeply. Nicholas was a man who needed her, needed what she had to give, what she wanted to give.

When she watched him leave a while later she vowed she would find a way to help him.

Even if it meant confronting a ghost.

9

THE FOLLOWING DAY went by in a blur of activity. A shipment of new stock came in that had to be unpacked, priced and displayed. The postcard announcements she'd mailed out brought in a lot of customers, eager to take advantage of the ten percent off she was giving on first purchases. She even ran out of her signature wrapping paper.

But when the rush was over and Ali turned the sign in the window to Closed, her mind was not on the promising start-up of her new shop. It was on her decision.

"And you're going to help me," Ali said, stopping to stroke Kashka, who was curled up in a large teddy bear's lap. "You're my way in."

Kashka purred and stretched.

"Don't get any ideas about going anywhere, kitty. I have a can of tuna with your name on it. You can eat while I get ready."

Kashka gave Ali her full attention when she heard the whir of the electric can opener, rubbing Ali's legs and nearly tripping her when she put the tuna down. Ali went upstairs to change.

She dressed casually, choosing her white Victorian nightgown as the first layer. Over it she pulled a long, full, soft denim skirt that buttoned up the front. The white flounced hem of the nightgown peeked beneath the skirt and she left its buttons undone to the knee. The top of the nightgown served as a camisole, to which she added her blue chambray shirt, leaving it unbuttoned, too.

Slipping her feet into a pair of white leather moccasins and grabbing her shoulder bag, Ali headed back downstairs to pick up her unwilling prop.

Kashka was licking the empty dish of tuna as if she hadn't eaten in days. She didn't seem pleased to be picked up, but Ali had a plan and Kashka had as little chance as Nicholas of evading it. With the mewing cat in her embrace, Ali set out for the Knight mansion on her mission.

She couldn't fight what she didn't know, so she was going to have to get past Nicholas's defenses. The first step was to chink away at his armor until she exposed the man she'd seen last night, the wildly gorgeous, yet vulnerable human.

His stand against that lout Billy Lawrence had shown her his chivalrous side, even if he had interfered in a problem she could have handled.

The man she was falling in love with was the man behind the cool exterior.

Tonight she was going to break through his defenses by ignoring them; iron gate, brooding mansion, cool aloofness. He wouldn't be expecting her, and surprise was the best offense of all. Her plan had to succeed because she had a future planned for him...them...once she dragged him kicking and screaming out of the past—once she found the reason for its hold on him.

When she reached the Knight mansion, Ali stood outside the imposing gate, stroking the cat in her arms. Then she gathered her courage and went in to rescue her chivalrous, dark and stormy knight.

NICHOLAS LAY stretched on the sofa in the library, a newspaper across his chest as he dozed. The thudding of the solid brass knocker woke him. He ignored it, turning onto his side and trying to recapture the dream he'd been having. In it Ms. Charbonneau was behind the dressing screen in her new shop slipping into something more comfortable.

The knocking persisted, and he yelled, "Go away!"

Whoever it was didn't take the hint. They continued slapping the knocker against the door, insisting on being recognized.

"All right, all right. I'm coming." Nicholas got up from the sofa with a groan, determined to dispatch the unwelcome intruder quickly.

When he reached the hall, he yanked open the door. "I said go awa—" Nicholas stopped in mid warning when he saw who was standing before him. Had he conjured her up with his dreaming? He was going to have to be more careful about these fantasies. She didn't have the sense God gave a goose, or she would stay away from him.

"I came to return your cat," Ali said, stroking the squirming feline.

"She doesn't appear to want to be returned," Nicholas said, taking the cat from her, nonetheless, and setting Kashka free to roam the mansion. "Go catch a mouse."

Ali's eyes swept the foyer with its magnificent staircase and marble floors . . . and layers of dust. "I doubt there are any mice to be found," she said with a laugh.

"Why not?"

Ali glanced at the chandelier above a pedestal table. It was draped with spiderwebs of amazing intricacy.

"Because," Ali said, "I suspect the spiders have probably eaten them all."

"Is there something I can do for you?" he asked, not bothering to veil his impatience. He was in no mood for her games. He hadn't had much sleep. *Her* ghost had been in the ruins again last night. Funny how Ali's arrival in Stonebriar had stirred everything up. It had been a long time since the ghost had been so active.

"I love these old mansions, you know," Ali said, sailing inside and continuing her chatter, so he couldn't get in a word to discourage her. "It must be just heaven to live in one."

"No. It isn't. You wouldn't like it, trust me. If you don't mind . . . I was busy." He wanted her to go. Or at least he should want her to go.

"Don't be ridiculous," Ali said, tossing her long blond hair over her shoulder and ignoring his comment. "How could someone not love something so beautiful?"

"It's old, drafty, and falling down around my ears, that's why. You're romanticizing it. It's just a house."

"It wouldn't be just a house if I lived in it," Ali said, venturing farther inside. "Why don't you fix the house up and return it to its former glory? It must have been really something when it was new."

"That would take a great deal of money."

"A place this size and you don't have money?"

She had nerve, he'd give her that. "The family money... is gone. There was a little problem with the stock market."

"I'm sorry." Ali was contrite. "I shouldn't have said that. Sometimes I don't think before I speak. You know, there must be a way you could...I know, you could do tours to get the money to restore this place. And I could be the trial run. What do you think?"

"What do I think? Tours...are you nuts? I don't want..."

"What's through this door?" Ali asked, cutting him off and moving to begin the tour.

Nicholas helplessly followed, pantomiming strangling her behind her back. She stopped abruptly and they collided. Why did she have to smell so damn good? His hands went up to steady her, then just as quickly dropped away, as if he'd touched something that was forbidden.

"What... why did you stop like that? What are you doing?" he sputtered, his mood bordering on the homicidal.

"Did anyone ever tell you you're *real* cranky?"

"Cranky? Cranky! You invade my privacy and explore my house as if you're on some kind of acid scavenger hunt, and because I'm trying to throw you out, I'm cranky?"

"What's down this way?" Ali asked. "I've already seen the library."

"The dining room," Nicholas answered as she walked past him. Nicholas followed her doggedly. "Look, I think—" he began again in exasperation.

"Guess you don't entertain much, huh?" Ali said, trailing her finger in the thick layer of dust on the Chippendale dining table. "What a shame. If I lived here, I would have dinner parties with a fire lit," she said, going to look at the fireplace with built-in shelves on either side. Empty shelves. The whole house was empty.

"Do you always frown?" Ali asked, looking up.

"Yes. Are you done now?"

"What about over the mantel?" Ali asked.

"What about it?" What was she talking about now? Her conversation bounced around like a Ping-Pong ball on the loose.

"What would you put over it?"

"Nothing. I like it with nothing over it, the way it is now."

"Not me. I'd put a painting over it. Maybe one of your paintings...."

"My what?"

"Your paintings. Jessica mentioned you used to be a painter."

"Jessica is a busybody," Nicholas grumbled. He left Ali standing in the dining room and returned to the library, where he stood before the piano, picking out a tune with one finger.

"Why do you resent me so?" Ali asked, rejoining him in the library.

Nicholas crashed his hands onto the keys. "What is it with all these questions?"

Ali shrugged. "I guess I just want to get to know you better," she said, going to the sofa and picking up the scattered newspapers and stacking them before sitting down.

"You know me." How on earth was he going to get rid of her?

"No. I don't. I don't think even Jessica knows you. She loves you, but she doesn't know you. You've built a thick wall around yourself."

"What are you, a shrink?" he asked, sitting down on the piano stool, his back to the piano. "No, you can't be a shrink, they don't go around giving out free advice."

"I'd like to be your friend," Ali said, sensing his need behind the stubbornness.

"I don't think so," he said, sounding uninterested.

"Why not?"

"Because I don't have any friends," he said without hesitation. As if he were proud of it.

"But that's so sad."

"Not if that's the way you want it." He lowered his gaze and dragged a hand through his dark hair.

"What about women?"

"Oh, I have those," Nicholas said, looking up and uttering a hollow laugh.

"Like Heather?" she inquired.

So she had ventured into his office—and stayed long enough to hear Heather leave that message on the answering machine. He'd wondered when he'd found her watch near the doorway.

"Like Heather," he agreed.

"I'd think that would get real boring."

Nicholas raised an eyebrow. "No, boring isn't a word I would use to describe Heather," he assured her.

"You know what I mean. I'm talking about a real relationship."

"Save me." Nicholas raised his eyes heavenward.

"I plan to," Ali muttered beneath her breath.

"What was that you said?"

"I said, were you planning to eat?"

"What? Now you're inviting yourself to dinner? Have you no manners at all?"

"Not when my stomach is growling. I got so busy in the shop today that I forgot to eat. Do you think you could possibly feed me?"

"I don't know. I'll have to see if Kashka's come up with that mouse."

"Thanks, but a cheese sandwich would suffice."

Nicholas rose from the piano bench. "I suppose you want me to make it and serve it to you, as well."

"I am feeling a little weak."

"I am feeling a little weak," he repeated mockingly; he headed down the hall to the kitchen. He wondered if she would search the library while he was gone. Would she even confine herself to the library? Either she was just naturally nosy or up to no good. Probably both.

"Debutantes are supposed to have better manners," he muttered to himself, removing the makings for grilled cheese sandwiches from the refrigerator. Unlike the rest of the house, the kitchen was spotless. Lucky for her she'd picked the one thing he knew how to cook other than a peanut butter sandwich.

He tried to listen for Ali's movements, but the kitchen was too far from the library to hear properly. Instead he hurried and returned to the library with the sandwiches and wine for their impromptu dinner.

She was sitting where he'd left her on the sofa. But he wouldn't bet the family silver, assuming there'd been any, that she'd been there the whole time. He suspected she practiced that innocent look of hers in the mirror every morning.

"It smells wonderful," Ali said when he set the tray on the cocktail table before her.

"Let's have a toast first," Nicholas suggested, handing her a glass of wine.

"What shall we toast to?" Ali asked, slipping off her white moccasins and tucking her bare feet beneath her on the sofa.

"To the success of your business," Nicholas suggested, leaning forward and clinking his glass with hers.

She cast a quick, puzzled glance at him and took a sip of wine. "But I thought you wanted my business to fail."

"No. I wanted you to leave Stonebriar."

"I'm not going," she assured him, picking up the cheese sandwich and biting into its warmth.

"I've accepted that."

"See, then maybe we can be friends."

"I said I accepted it, not that I liked the idea." Nicholas picked up his sandwich and began eating. The silence stretched between them. Finally when Nicholas had finished his sandwich, he spoke again. "Why are you so determined to stay in Stonebriar?"

"Because of my father. I want to prove to him that I can take care of myself. That I don't need him or a husband. He's got this stubborn notion that I will work in the family business until I'm safely married."

"I take it you don't want to marry."

"Maybe. But not until I'm ready. And not a man my father picks out for me. I want to be in love.... I want to choose...."

Nicholas's laugh was dark. "You never choose whom you fall in love with."

Ali looked at her empty wineglass. She picked it up and peered at Nicholas through it. "My glass is empty. You're not being a very good host," she said, handing it to him.

"I'm not being a very good host? May I remind you that you weren't invited here?" he said, refilling her glass. "If you check your book of manners, you'll see that if I didn't invite you, I'm not obligated to entertain you."

"You're such a stickler for rules, aren't you?" she observed, taking the glass. "What do you do for entertainment around here, anyway?"

"Read the newspaper."

"I noticed, and play the piano, right? Besides that?"

Nicholas shrugged. "I go into the city."

"Don't you have any games we could play?" she asked, deftly avoiding the subject of the city... and women he could meet there.

"Games?" he asked, thinking they were probably in the midst of one of her inventions at the moment. And since it was her game, he couldn't tell if he was winning or losing. Losing would be the safer bet.

"Like Monopoly."

He shook his head.

"Scrabble."

No again.

"Cards ... anything?"

"No."

"I've got it," she said, snapping her fingers. "I know a game we can play that doesn't require cards, a board or anything."

"What? What are you talking about?"

"Madonna's game," Ali answered, smiling with pleasure.

"*Madonna's game?*" Nicholas looked at her askance. "I don't even want to know...."

How, he wondered, had things degenerated this rapidly? When had he completely lost control of the situation? It didn't take a genius to reflect that it had been when he'd opened the door and let her enter his home.

"It's called Truth or Dare."

"I've never heard of it. Really, like I told you, I'm busy...."

"The game is very simple, really," Ali said, ignoring him. "We each get to ask the other a question and we have to answer the question with the honest truth. If we don't, then it's agreed we take the dare."

"What kind of game is that?"

"I get to go first."

"I told you ... why do you get to go first?"

"Because it was my idea," Ali explained, smiling with sweet pretended innocence.

"Forget it. I don't know why I'm even ... I'm *not* playing any of your—"

"Why don't you paint anymore?" Ali's question stopped his objection cold.

"That's easy. The truth is I'm not any good," Nicholas answered shortly. "Game's over." Picking up the plates and his empty wineglass, he headed for the hall.

Ali was not to be dissuaded that easily, however. She picked up her own glass, drained it, then followed him.

"You've asked your question. Now I think you should leave," he said over his shoulder.

"Want to know what I think?" Ali asked when they reached the kitchen.

"No."

"I think you're wrong. After all, Jessica told me you had talent. Maybe you should give your painting another chance. You must miss it."

Nicholas set the plates in the sink with his glass, then turned to face her. "Jessica wants to believe I can still paint, but whatever talent I might have once had is gone."

"You mean to tell me in all this time you haven't been tempted just once to try again?" Ali asked in disbelief.

Nicholas leaned against the sink and crossed his arms in front of him.

"You haven't painted *anything?*" Ali persisted. "Don't you have any more of this wine?" She walked to the refrigerator and peered inside. "Nope. Where do you hide it? You really are a terrible host."

"You don't need any more wine."

"I'm perfectly fine. Wine doesn't make me tipsy."

"It makes you nosy."

"No. I'm naturally nosy. I have been since I was a kid. My parents had to lock their bedroom door." Ali's hand flew over her lips. "Oops. Shouldn't have said that. Say, you never did answer my question."

Nicholas studied her a moment, considering. Maybe he did know how to make her go home.

10

"I HAVE BEEN working on a painting," Nicholas admitted. He rubbed his fingertips along his stubbled chin as his eyes studied her, watching for her reaction. "Would you like to see it?"

"Ah, sure . . ." Ali agreed, caught off guard by his conciliatory attitude. She recalled the slashed painting she'd found in his office and wondered if maybe now wouldn't be a good time to leave, after all. Was Nicholas finally coming around, or was he leading her to the secret room in Bluebeard's castle? Sometimes it was hard to decide if having a lively imagination was a blessing or a curse.

"You're certain you want to?"

"Of course. Why wouldn't I want to? But if you're having second thoughts, you don't have to. . . ."

"No, come along. . . ."

Ali trailed down the hall after Nicholas to the entry foyer and then up the sweeping staircase to the south wing, where she stood waiting while he lit several candles and placed them around the room to illuminate the cavernous space.

"Why don't you just turn on the light?" she asked, spying a switch near the door.

"It's broken."

The soft glow of candlelight revealed an assortment of shapes in the darkness. Concentrating, Ali realized she was in the room Nicholas used to work out his demons. There was a wide array of gym equipment. Near the window stood what appeared to be an easel with a canvas on it. A cloth was tossed over the canvas, obscuring it from her view.

"I thought you wanted to see?" Nicholas asked when she remained in the doorway.

"I do."

"Then come closer."

Said the spider to the fly. She was both attracted and wary of the attraction.

Giving in to her curiosity, she moved to join him by the easel.

"Ready?" he asked.

She nodded.

His face was a careful mask of unconcern; he lifted the edge of the cloth and yanked it from the canvas.

Ali was quiet as she stared at the painting. It was a portrait of a nude. She knew that Nicholas wanted her to be shocked.

She was the portrait's subject.

So that explained what he'd been doing when she'd heard him moving around up here, the night he'd carried her from the property next door. He'd been washing paintbrushes, readying them and dragging the easel out of storage, placing it near the window in preparation for painting her. It hadn't been a dream, after all.

"You aren't saying anything." Nicholas's deep, rich voice invaded her thoughts. "Are you shocked to the tips of your debutante toes?"

"How do you know I'm a debutante?" she asked, evading the real question. She continued studying the painting while trying to decide what she was going to say to him.

Nicholas shrugged. "Caroline...Billy...it isn't hard to tell. Besides, Jessica mentioned it."

"It's a cop-out."

"I wouldn't be so hard on yourself...."

"No. I'm talking about your painting," she said. He had painted her so that her long blond hair hid her charms. The painting hid his feelings, as well. She wasn't an expert, but even she could see that while it was technically good, the portrait lacked life.

"A cop-out?" Nicholas repeated, eyeing Ali narrowly.

Ali nodded, biting her lip. It was clear that he had been prepared for outrage, not judgment.

"I don't know what you're talking about," Nicholas said, his dark eyes avoiding hers.

"I think you do," she countered. "But if you'll get me a glass of wine, I'll explain."

Nicholas looked as though he wanted to say something, but instead stood studying the painting. Had he painted it to exorcise her or someone else? Was he angry because it hadn't worked?

A few minutes later he returned with her glass of wine.

She took it and drank a few sips.

"You were going to explain what's wrong with my painting," Nicholas reminded her coldly.

Ali nodded, then moved around the room, looking at the various pieces of workout equipment that shared the room with his painting. She trailed her finger along a padded weight bench; an impressive number of weights were suspended on the bar over it. There was no dust on the bench, which wasn't a surprise; his finely honed body provided proof of its regular use.

Under his watchful eye, she finally returned to the painting, handing him her empty wineglass.

"I think it's better that I show you. Do you have a fresh canvas?"

"Yes, but—"

"Get it," she instructed, lifting the one he'd painted from the easel.

When he returned with the fresh canvas, she had him put it upon the easel.

"I still don't . . ."

"Just watch, okay? Don't say anything."

Holding his puzzled gaze, she kicked off her soft white moccasins and began shedding her clothing. First came the chambray shirt, then the skirt, until she stood before him in nothing but her sleeveless, white Victorian nightgown and her panties.

"Not that I'm objecting," Nicholas said, finding his voice. "But what the hell are you doing?"

Ali lifted a forefinger to her lips in a request for silence.

He threw up his hands in a gesture of defeat, remaining silent and watchful as she unbuttoned the tiny pearl buttons at the neck of the sheer cotton gown and let it, too, fall, pooling at her feet.

She saw him swallow as her panties followed suit. Gathering her long, blond hair, she piled it on top of her head, fashioning a topknot. That done, she issued her challenge.

"Now paint me. Not a woman from the past—not a lifeless creature—but me, a woman with passion in her blood."

"I can't," he said, almost choking.

"Why not?" Ali asked, insecurity momentarily rearing its head, making her feel every vulnerable inch of her nakedness.

"Because when I look at you—"

"But you're not looking at me."

His eyes impaled her then, burning and hot. "I can't think when I look at you, okay?"

"But don't you understand? That's exactly my point! Don't think. *Feel.* Can't you see what's wrong with your painting? The artistic quality is there, but you paint without passion. Your work is cold and distant, without feeling."

He reached out his hand, placing it in the small of her back, skin touching skin.

She didn't flinch at his touch, nor did she move toward him.

"Come closer," he said, this time a much more dangerous spider addressing the fly.

"But aren't you going to paint me?"

"Later...."

"Later?"

He nodded. "First I must find just how high your passion burns."

There was just the slightest pressure of the hand on her back, coaxing her.

She slipped into his embrace.

"Why did you come here tonight?" he whispered.

"Nicholas?"

"Mmm...?"

"Shut up and kiss me."

"Since you insist," he murmured, proceeding to do her bidding. As their tongues dueled, he slid his hands to curve her bottom, lifting and pressing her to his straining arousal. Nuzzling her throat, he whispered those same maddening words of encouragement she remembered from the picnic. Though a masculine version, his imagination was as dark and as rich as her own. She had met her match...her soul mate.

Backing up, he maneuvered them to the weight bench, where he seated himself, pulling her down to straddle his lap. He whispered her name, rubbing her against him until small, exquisite moans started in her throat and escaped through her parted lips. His teasing kisses across her closed eyes were as light as butterfly wings.

"My turn," she said, opening her eyes and pulling him to his feet. Standing behind him, she wrapped her arms around him and slid her hands beneath his soft polo shirt, her hands foraging in a leisurely perusal of his chest. The soft mat of hair was warm and she ran her fingers through it, teasing his nipples with her nails.

He reached back with his hands to cup her buttocks, his long fingers separating, exploring, teasing in their turn. They were a perfect match in height. Her face was nestled in his hair, she could smell the faint scent of his shampoo. She nibbled at the tip of his ear, whispering wildly improbable suggestions. The whole while she inched up his shirt, provocatively rubbing her breasts against his back.

He pulled her around to face him and she pushed his arms above his head, tugging his shirt free, the action arching her body, thus offering her pretty neck and up-turned breasts to his warm mouth.

Her hands attacked his belt, urgently unbuckling it and pulling it from his pants.

"Wait." Nicholas stepped back, toeing off his loafers. "Better let me do this," he said, giving her a smiling grimace. "With your haste it could be painful." Unbuttoning his pants, he gingerly worked the zipper down, then kicked his pants and briefs free.

Ali reached out a hand to touch his eagerness, finding the evidence of his desire thrilling, exciting. She gloried in the trembling her caress elicited. There could be no denying his body wanted her, even if his mind did not.

Puckering her lips, she slid to her knees and kissed her way to the tip of him. Her hands gripped his lean hips, and she began taking him into her mouth with smooth, even strokes.

He buried his hand into her hair on a strangled groan, loosening her topknot. She could feel the shuddering response in his strong thighs, felt his hands clench in her hair.

And then he was pulling her to her feet.

"I want to be inside you," he said, leading her back to the weight bench and positioning her across its length. "Put your hands on the weight bar above you. Yes, like that. Now wrap your fingers around it and hold on tight."

The feel of the round metal bar beneath her fingers was hard and erotic. Ali looked up at Nicholas, admiring his lean strength. Candlelight licked his body, worshiping his perfection. Ali felt her body move involuntarily, anxious for his touch. He looked at her and little thrills eddied through her blood, sending it to the boiling point. She wanted this, wanted him...oh, how she wanted him!

He came to her then, straddling the narrow bench. Parting her legs, he pulled her bottom into his lap. And then his long fingers began their delicate, expert seduction. "Do you like that?" he asked, his voice a hoarse whisper.

Her eyes were closed, her breathing rapid.

"Do you?" he demanded, increasing the pressure and her pleasure.

"Yes, please."

"Oh, so polite. We're going to have to do something about your debutante manners. What a hell of a time for you to recover them. Repeat after me," he instructed, proceeding to say the most outrageously sexy things she'd ever heard.

"I can't say that," Ali objected, a little shocked.

"Sure you can," he assured her, stilling his hand. "If you want me to continue, that is. Come on, say it," he coaxed, a wicked chuckle escaping his full lips while his fingers toyed with her, granting her pleasure and then stopping, teasing. . . .

She remained silent.

"Oh, a stubborn case. . . ." There was a note of accepted challenge in his voice; he lowered his head, whispering soft kisses down the slope of her abdomen, his stubble both tickling and arousing.

Ali let out a half gasp at the feel of his warm tongue when he began his campaign of tantalizing provocation; he was seducing her!

Her capitulation was embarrassingly immediate, but she was beyond caring. Responding with wild abandon to his delicious torment, she repeated his words, even inventing a few shocking phrases of her own.

"My, my, my. . . and you a debutante," Nicholas teased. He rose to position himself. His hands cupped her breasts, squeezing gently as he filled her with a slow, slow thrust. "Look at me, Ali," he demanded, his excruciatingly indolent lovemaking driving her to move her head from side to side, while her body coaxed him to thrust with ever quickening desire.

She opened her eyes.

His face was dark with passion, his eyes glittering with the flames of emotional fires long banked. He built the intensity of their loving, controlling the tempo until Ali cried out his name.

"If this is madness, let it claim me," Nicholas vowed passionately, exploding while Ali writhed beneath him. Tears dripped from his long lashes to mingle with the sweat from their soaked bodies.

She felt his fingers bite into her shoulders; then he lost control completely, his body arching bowlike until he was spent.

"Sweet witch," he murmured, looking down at her, his breathing ragged, his eyes slumberous, his smile one of contented wonder.

11

ALI LOOKED UP at the heavenly-blue tray ceiling of the Knight mansion's master bedroom, where she lay beside Nicholas in a huge, fruitwood four-poster bed.

She'd really gone and done it this time.

Tonight she'd either done the smartest or the dumbest thing in her life. She smiled contentedly and sighed. It sure felt right.

A glance around the large, dusty room showed her the clothes she'd carried from the studio were now tossed over a chintz-covered chair next to a massive desk. The desk's surface was untidy; a clutter of unopened mail, magazines and three empty shot glasses. The bottle of good Scotch to one side of the desk, however, was nearly full.

She should get up, get dressed and leave. Time...she needed time to think about what had happened.

"Why are you eyeing my desk? You thinking about rifling it or cleaning it?" Nicholas asked from the depth of his pillow.

"Neither. I'm not that obsessive...or nosy."

There was a snort of laughter muffled by the pillow.

"What?" Ali demanded, hitting his shoulder.

Nicholas opened one eye. "You, my dear, are under a huge misconception, for you are undoubtedly the most obsessively nosy woman I have ever met."

"Okay, so I'm curious by nature," she said, pouting.

His grunt was one of satisfaction at being right.

She glanced at him, only to see his eyes were closed. Gingerly she lifted the antique coverlet, gazing at her nakedness and the red marks Nicholas's stubble had left in their night of uninhibited lovemaking.

The night they'd spent in his studio in the south wing had been wildly exciting.

True, he hadn't spoken those three little words, but that had been because he'd been so busy with all the other provocative expressions he used so well.

She smiled, remembering all the other words he'd strung together while they'd made love. Making love in silence would never appeal to her again. He was a consummate lover, painting hot, sexy word images upon the willing canvas of her imagination. He could have brought her to completion without even touching her.

Oh, but his touch!

"Guess we gave a whole new meaning to the term workout bench,'" Nicholas said, making her drop the coverlet guiltily.

He was grinning wryly when she looked at him. She'd thought he'd fallen asleep.

Ali smiled at him, turning on her side to trail a finger over his full bottom lip. It was wonderful to see him relaxed, almost boyish. When she asked him the questions she had to ask, would he retreat to the defense of his distant aloofness?

No matter, she had to ask. If they were to go forward, he would have to put the past behind him.

"Nicholas . . ." she began, taking a deep breath, fearing to destroy the tender mood between them, but driven to know the truth.

"Mmm . . ." he murmured contentedly, his hand playing with the spill of her blond hair on the pillow.

"Will you tell me about . . . Camilla . . . about the fire . . . ?"

His hand stilled.

He looked away from her and up at the ceiling. "I suppose Jessica told you."

Ali was quick to defend Jessica. She didn't want to put a breach between them. "Jessica didn't tell me until recently. It wasn't until I—"

"You what?" He looked back at her.

She bit her bottom lip. "Until I discovered the slashed painting of Camilla in your office. It gave me such a shock. I thought the painting was of me."

He removed his hand from her hair, clearly beginning to distance himself. "Why didn't you ask me about the painting?"

"Because I was embarrassed my curiosity had gotten the better of me. And I was—well, the painting *was* slashed."

"What has Jessica told you exactly?"

"Only that there was a fire fifteen years ago at Hawthorne House that destroyed it, killing your father, as well as Camilla Hawthorne."

"And the ensuing scandal. Jessica must have told you about that," he said, stacking his hands behind his head, a muscle clenching in his lean jaw.

"Yes," Ali agreed. "She did. Jessica explained there were rumors, but that they were just that and nothing more."

Nicholas smiled. "That sounds like Jessica. She likes to believe the best of everyone, probably even believes Joe Allen will someday show up on time. But I'm afraid the truth in this case is even more damning than the rumors. You see, I'm the only one who knows the truth."

His eyes took on a faraway look again as he began recalling the painful past.

"The Hawthornes and the Knights have been neighbors here since my grandfather and Camilla's bought the land and built these mansions all those years ago. Back then the mansions were built as summer houses for the families to escape the heat of the city. The two men were successful businessmen and best friends."

"Do you remember your grandfather?"

Nicholas shook his head. "No. The stock market crash of '29 came a few years after the two men built here in the flush of their careers. My grandfather was a stockbroker. He committed suicide in the library of the Knight mansion."

"How awful," Ali said, moving closer to Nicholas to offer him comfort.

"My grandfather had a son, as did Camilla's grandfather. Her grandfather became a substitute father for my father, as the two boys grew up. In later years they became estranged."

"Do you know why?" Ali asked, propping up her head with her hand and bent elbow.

"Camilla's father lost a great deal of money the year she turned eighteen. My father was a stockbroker, like my grandfather, and Camilla's father claimed my father conned him into investing in a bad stock deal. Camilla's mother and father were killed later that year in a boating accident."

"Were you and Camilla friends?"

"No, not really. We knew each other, of course, but she was five years older than I. My father paid to send her to a good college. He also bought the Hawthorne House when it came up for auction, allowing Camilla's grandfather to live there until he died, during her senior year of college. Camilla then lived there once she graduated."

"There's something I don't understand. If you and Camilla weren't friends, then how did you come to paint her portrait?"

Nicholas was silent for some time. "We were lovers," he said finally.

"Oh."

"It's in the past, Ali. Jessica doesn't know about it. No one does."

"Why? Neither of you were married. Why did you hide the fact that—was it just because Camilla was older?"

Nicholas shrugged his shoulders. "It was Camilla's wish to keep it a secret, and I was so infatuated with her, I would have done anything she asked. Remember she was an older woman of twenty-five to my twenty. She seduced me."

"I don't think I want to hear this," Ali said, a pang of jealousy hitting her.

"You asked. Besides, I want you to know the truth about what happened. It was Camilla who encouraged my painting by finding a gallery to give me my first showing. I was painting her portrait as a thank-you. It was to be a surprise.

"She had the rest of my paintings at Hawthorne House because she was arranging the framing."

"And your paintings were all destroyed in the fire?"

Nicholas nodded. "Yes. The only painting left was the portrait that was still here in my studio, the one you found slashed in my office."

"But I don't understand. Why did you slash the painting if you and Camilla were—?"

Nicholas closed his eyes tightly.

"That night of the fire I had been to the gallery, and the gallery owner had told me he'd arranged for an important art critic to be at my showing. I stopped by Hawthorne House to tell Camilla my news.

"But when I arrived at Hawthorne House I heard a violent argument upstairs. I ran up to defend Camilla, but was stopped short when I heard my father's voice coming from her bedroom.

"He was shouting at her, telling her he had no intention of leaving my mother to marry her. It was then that Camilla icily informed him that she was pregnant with his child.

"And then she told him that I fancied myself in love with her, that we were also lovers."

"What happened?"

"My father refused to believe her."

Nicholas's laugh was hollow. "But Camilla was ready for him. She told him that when she'd found out she was pregnant by him, she'd purposely set out to seduce me to make sure one of us would marry her.

"She taunted him, telling him she would tell me the baby was mine, that one way or another she would get back what our family had stolen from hers."

"You can't continue to blame yourself," Ali said, seeing that he did. "She must have been very sick."

Nicholas continued as if he hadn't heard her. "Camilla didn't love my father. She didn't love me, either. She'd seduced us both as an act of revenge. Her father's hatred had poisoned her."

"What happened? Did you leave?"

"Yes. My pride was shredded to ribbons. I couldn't stand to hear any more. When I left they were still arguing. I ran down the stairs and drove into the city. There I spent the night with a woman who was a complete stranger.

"When I returned home the next day, it was to find my life destroyed. My father and Camilla were dead. My mother might as well have been. The flames that had consumed Hawthorne House had consumed my family, the paintings that were my future and the life-blood of my talent."

"Oh, Nicholas, I'm so very sorry." Ali reached out to touch him, but he turned away, still not ready to be comforted.

"Did they ever find a cause of the fire?" she asked, trying to keep him talking. Trying to help him heal.

"No. No one will ever know what really happened. The rumors at the time claimed my father had killed Camilla and then committed suicide like my grandfather—but nothing was ever proven."

"Do you think that's what happened?"

"I don't know. It's certainly possible. Now do you understand why I've wanted you to leave Stonebriar from the first, that I knew the two of us would come to this . . . that I could. . . ."

"Could what?"

"Love you."

12

ALI LOOKED AT NICHOLAS. Having told her his story, they'd made love...slowly, tenderly; then he'd fallen into a light sleep, unburdened.

She couldn't sleep. Restless, she got up and pulled on her nightgown.

The library drew her downstairs.

She walked around the room. She stopped before an antique music stand and wondered if Nicholas's mother had loved music. Had she played the piano and taught Nicholas? Ali fingered the keys. So much sadness. It was as if the Knight family had been cursed.

She went to stand at the French doors that looked out to the spot where Hawthorne House had once stood. Just as she was about to turn away, she saw it. The ghostly woman in white walking amid the ruins.

Acting on impulse, Ali opened the French doors and slipped outside.

"Ali..." Nicholas's voice drifted from upstairs as she stood in the chilly night air.

Knowing he would try to stop her, she headed for the specter, determined once and for all to see it up close.

"*Ali...no!*" This time Nicholas's voice was urgent.

She looked over her shoulder to see him silhouetted in the master bedroom window. Ignoring his plea, she began to run, heedless of the danger.

She had the strangest feeling the ghost was calling to her, trying to tell her something. But what? And would it only disappear once again when she reached Hawthorne House?

"Ali, stop. . . ." She could hear Nicholas running behind her.

Increasing her speed, Ali ran at full tilt across the dewy grass. She slipped and stumbled near the ruins, but caught herself. She had a sense that she must find out what the ghost wanted tonight, or the opportunity would be lost to her forever.

Glancing behind her, she saw Nicholas; he was hopping up and down on one foot and swearing. He'd pulled on a pair of jeans but was shirtless and barefoot.

Turning back to her mission, her heart fell when she saw the ghost had vanished.

She was too late!

Ali stepped into the ruins, her spirits sinking.

"Please, come back," she pleaded. "Help me. . ." She didn't know what she was asking for, only that the ghost was trying to tell her something.

She began to get an eerie feeling and sensed someone standing behind her. Summoning her meager courage, she turned and let out a gasp of surprise.

It was like looking into a mirror. The woman in white looked exactly like her.

A sense of unreality seized Ali and she moved forward to touch what she saw, wanting to establish that the woman existed and was not a figment of her overactive imagination.

When her hand moved right through the figure, Ali jumped back.

The eyes of the woman in white beseeched her. Ali knew she was trying to communicate, but couldn't understand.

"Tell me somehow. What is it?" Ali cried.

But as she stood there pleading, the figure in white began to fade. When Nicholas caught up with her, it was gone.

"What are you doing out here? You could have hurt yourself," Nicholas scolded, coming up behind her and pulling her into his arms.

"I saw her, Nicholas."

"Who?" he asked, frowning.

"Camilla."

"Camilla is dead."

"I know that. I saw her . . . her ghost."

"Ali . . ."

"I saw her," she insisted.

Nicholas sighed. "I know."

"You've seen her too, haven't you?" Ali asked, pulling back and looking up at him.

"Yes," he admitted with reluctance. "I've seen her for the past fifteen years. Sometimes she's more active than others—the times when my mood is the darkest. And then at other times I'll come to believe she's gone for good, only to see her once again. She always comes back."

"Why? What does she want?"

His dark eyes were hooded.

"Nicholas?"

"Me. She wants me."

"What?"

"She wants me to join her in death."

Ali stared at him. "Why would she want that? You didn't kill her."

He looked away from her, staring off into the distance. "I might have."

"What are you talking about?"

Nicholas turned. In his eyes she saw the wasted years of tormented doubt. Mirrored there were his worst fears. His voice was eerily soft and distracted as he explained. "I can't remember." He rubbed his eyes with his fists, as if to clear his vision of the past. "I can't remember anything I did that night after I left Hawthorne House. My memory is hazy from the time I left until I returned the next day with a monumental hangover. The cause of the fire was never determined. I can't be certain that at some point I didn't come back and set the fire out of rage . . . grief . . . revenge."

"You've been living with that fear all these years, haven't you?" Ali said with sudden understanding.

He shrugged.

"It's the reason you hide from your emotions, isn't it?"

He didn't answer her, but the stricken look on his face gave away the truth.

Ali experienced an overwhelming feeling of joy at the fact that he had allowed himself to feel again with her, that she had been the one to reach him. She had to ask. "Why did you take a chance on me?"

His voice was low and husky as he answered. "I'd say it was rather the other way around, wouldn't you?"

Ali smiled. "Lucky for you I'm the impulsive sort, then, isn't it?"

"And nosy...don't forget nosy," he said, teasing, still new to the feelings she was trying to draw from him.

She raised her chin. "Being nosy gets one's questions answered. For example, why haven't you razed the ruins of Hawthorne House? Why have you let them remain?"

Nicholas pondered her question. "I recall reading once that Cole Porter loved his wife so much that when she died, he burned their house to the ground because he couldn't bear to remember what he'd lost. I left the ruins of Hawthorne House for the opposite reason. I didn't want to forget what happened."

"But that keeps you living in the past," Ali observed; she walked about the ruins, finally coming back to stop in front of what remained of the fireplace.

"What are you doing?" Nicholas asked when she started exploring the remaining stones.

"I don't know. Something is bothering me. Every time I've seen Camilla's ghost it's been standing by the fireplace. Have you noticed?"

Nicholas shrugged.

"She always makes her way to this fireplace, as if she's leading me to it, trying to tell me something. It's always where she disappears."

"You know, you're right," Nicholas agreed.

"Maybe there is something here," Ali suggested. "Something she wants us to find."

"I don't know, Ali. That's a pretty farfetched conclusion, even for you."

"Maybe, but I'm determined to check it out, anyway," she vowed, beginning to investigate the stones.

"Be careful," he said, when a stone fell, nearly hitting her bare foot. "Here, let me help you."

In a half hour they'd gone over the remains of the fireplace without finding anything. "That's that," Nicholas said, helping her up.

"I guess so," Ali agreed, not hiding her disappointment. "Maybe tomorrow when it's light we can..."

"Okay, but for now I think we should go back inside. We both need a bath," he said, dusting the dirt from his hands and wiping them on his muscled thighs.

"Meow..." Kashka darted forward, running between Ali's legs and unbalancing her. Ali stumbled.

"Careful," Nicholas said, jumping forward to help her keep her balance.

"Ouch!"

"What's the matter? Did you hurt your foot? You shouldn't be out here barefoot, anyway."

"I stepped on something."

"Here, let me have a look." Nicholas bent down to check her foot. "No, it's okay. There isn't a scratch or anything. Let me see if I can feel around for what you stepped on," he said, concerned.

"Aha, this must be it." He stood with something in his hand.

"What it it? I hope it isn't rusty. I hate shots," Ali said squeamishly.

"No, don't worry. It's . . . it must have been in the fireplace, and you dislodged it when you stumbled," Nicholas surmised, studying a blackened key in the moonlight.

"That's it, don't you see? The key must be what Camilla wanted us to find."

"I don't know, Ali. . . ."

"It's an odd place for a key, even you have to admit that. I wonder what it fits."

"I doubt we'll ever know. If it fitted anything in Hawthorne House, it would have been burned in the fire."

"Can I have the key?"

"Sure," he said, dropping it into her open hand. "And no argument, we're going back inside," he informed her, scooping her into the crook of his arms.

"I can walk, Nicholas. My foot is fine, really."

"I know, but I like carrying you," he murmured.

Once inside, Nicholas ran a hot bath and they both peeled out of their grimy clothes to slip into the warm water, lazily soaking away the chill.

Ali was so tired, her eyes drifted closed and she dozed lightly.

A while later, Nicholas lifted her from the tub and dried her off with gentle tenderness. She murmured sleepily, but enjoyed his attentions. Carrying her to the big, soft bed, he tucked her in, bestowing a kiss upon her forehead.

He opened her hand to retrieve the key that was still clutched there. For a long time he stood by the window, looking over the ruins, while he turned the key in his hand.

Straightening, he returned the key to the nightstand. Going to his desk he opened a side drawer and removed a package wrapped in apricot paper. He carried it to the bed and laid it upon the nightstand beside the key.

Staring at Ali, he allowed himself the luxury of visualizing how she would look in lace and velvet—in the burgundy bodysuit—then headed for the south wing.

IN THE ENSUING WEEKS Attic Treasures flourished.

Ali even hired some local ladies to custom-make a line of bears for her shop. A local craftsman talked her into handling his hand-painted furniture as backdrops for her lingerie, and she was thinking of even starting a catalog for her shop.

Knight's Antiques floundered. More often than not the Closed sign was in the window. And when an item was sold it wasn't replaced. Dust was even starting to gather in the formerly spotless shop.

It was all Ali Charbonneau's fault, but this time Nicholas didn't mind.

For while Ali spent her days building up the clientele of Attic Treasures, Nicholas was to be found more often in the south wing of the Knight mansion than at Knight's Antiques.

Their nights were spent together in abandoned lovemaking, with Ali's love restoring life and hope to Nicholas. She coaxed him into beginning a collection for a gallery show.

Nicholas began to put aside his nagging fears and doubts; he could no longer force himself to send Ali away. He was hopelessly in love as he hadn't been since he was twenty.

Since that tragic night he couldn't remember.

Or maybe didn't want to.

"HELLO, JESSICA, it's good to see you," Ali said, looking up from the teddy bear she was dressing with a new item. "Haven't seen you in a while. Where've you been off to these past weeks?"

"Don't ask," Jessica answered, putting the back of her wrist to her forehead in a comical gesture. "My niece had twin baby girls and she already had twin two-year-old boys. I've been helping out and I don't mind telling you, I'm as pooped as I ever want to be."

"I can imagine—no, actually, I can't imagine *two* sets of twins," Ali said, putting the teddy bear back on display. "How will your niece ever manage?"

"With lots of help from the nanny my sister and I chipped in to give her for a year," Jessica said with a wink.

"Oh, Jessica, you're such a love. Gosh, I've missed talking with you. Why don't we have lunch at Thomure's? I've got to take inventory tonight, so I could use a break."

"I'd love it," Jessica agreed. "But first I promised to meet Nicholas at his shop. I'm treating myself to that Tiffany lamp of his I've been admiring for so long. Why don't you come with me? Then the two of us can persuade him to join us for lunch."

"Great idea. Just let me turn the Closed sign in the window and I'll be right with you," Ali agreed. "It'll be fun to play hooky for an hour or so."

"Good for you."

They took their time, stopping to window-shop as they strolled down the few blocks to Knight's Antiques. "I imagine Joe's caught you up on all the gossip," Ali said with a smile as they paused to admire a café table and a set of matching ice-cream-parlor chairs outside one shop.

"If you mean the fact that you and Nicholas have been keeping company, yes, he's told me about it. I couldn't be more pleased for Nicholas, and I love that you've got him painting again. I just hope for your sake you know what you're doing."

"Know what I'm doing?" Ali laughed as she spoke. "I never know what I'm doing. But I don't let it stop me, either."

Jessica shook her head and dabbed at her forehead with a frilly cotton handkerchief. "It's really humid out today. Must be a storm on the way."

"Well, here we are." Ali opened the door to Nicholas's shop.

Jessica went in first and Ali followed.

They could hear Nicholas on the telephone in his office, so the two of them stopped to admire the Tiffany lamp Jessica planned to purchase.

Ali ran her hand over the desk beneath the lamp. "This is a beautiful old desk, isn't it?" she said admiringly.

"Yes, it is," Nicholas said, joining them. "The desk belonged to Camilla's father."

"*What?*" Ali couldn't hide her surprise.

Nicholas shrugged. "Camilla asked me to refinish it for her about a month before the fire. I tried, but there's a deep scratch on the side that I couldn't eliminate. When I showed it to her, she asked me to dispose of the desk for her. I didn't have the heart to trash it, so later, when I opened the shop, I put it here. It hasn't sold because of the blemish, though. So what can I do for you ladies?"

"I've come to buy the Tiffany lamp," Jessica informed him, while Ali continued to study the dusty desk.

Nicholas smiled. "I knew I'd get you with it sooner or later. You almost lost it the other day. A young couple were pretty interested until they found out the price."

"Let's talk about that price, Nicholas."

"Uh-oh, I think I'm about to maybe break even," Nicholas said, picking up the lamp.

"Tell you what," Jessica said. "I'll pay full price for the lamp if you take Ali and me to lunch and pay for it."

"Deal," Nicholas said, heading toward his office with the lamp. "Just let me write this up for you."

"Nicholas, Jessica, come here!" Ali called from beside the desk.

"What is it?" they asked, rejoining her.

"The desk . . . I've discovered a false bottom . . . look!"

"I'll be damned!" Nicholas exclaimed, setting down the lamp and inspecting the keyhole Ali had revealed.

"Do you still have that key, Ali?" he asked.

Ali fished in her purse and retrieved the key from her wallet.

"Where did that key come from?" Jessica asked, puzzled.

"Ali discovered it in the ruins of Hawthorne House," Nicholas answered, fitting the key into the lock and turning it carefully. When he heard a click, he lifted the false lid.

Inside was a small black folder. Nicholas picked it up, opening it to study the contents.

"What is all that?" Ali asked.

Nicholas held up a hand. "Give me a minute to look this over. All I can tell at first glance is there are some stock certificates, a record of numbers of some sort and a letter."

The two women fidgeted impatiently as he studied the cache Ali had discovered. Finally he spoke again. "From the looks of this, it's possible Camilla's parents didn't die accidentally, after all. Given what seems to be the sizable amount of her father's gambling debts listed here and these worthless stock certificates, I'd wager they were murdered as an example, when these stocks he'd bought took a dive."

"Good heavens!" Jessica exclaimed.

"The letter . . . what does the letter say?" Ali asked.

Nicholas unfolded it and began reading. "It's from my father to Camilla's, telling him of the risk involved in the stock he wanted to buy and advising him against it."

"I told you, dear, you've been worrying yourself sick about your family for all these years, expecting the worst, and all for nothing," Jessica said.

Nicholas smiled at Jessica "I know you mean well, Jessica, but all this proves is that my family isn't larcenous. It says nothing about our tendency to violence."

"Nicholas." Jessica touched his arm soothingly. "No one knows what happened. . . ."

NICHOLAS HELD the paintbrushes under the faucet, watching the water blend the colors into a rainbow swirl of streams. Shaking the brushes to rid them of excess water, he brushed them across a soft, clean cloth, then upended them in a large jar, leaving them to dry.

He inhaled deeply as he stood before the large canvas he'd just completed. The smell of fresh paint was as appealing to him as the aroma of bread baking in the oven.

The painting he'd finished was one of Hawthorne House in all its glory before the fire. He hadn't thought he would paint it . . . could paint it. It was to be a part of a series he was doing. . . of all the old mansions along the river. While he hadn't planned to paint Hawthorne House, in the end he'd been compelled to. It was a part of the history of Stonebriar, his personal feelings aside.

Staring at his work, he wondered if other people felt as he did that houses had unique personalities, personalities not dictated by their owners. He smiled, thinking that perhaps houses and people had to fit for a home to be a success.

Some houses were as welcoming and comfortable as an old pair of shoes. Some were cold and foreboding. Other were mysterious and exciting. And rare ones were loving.

Houses even had a fragrance all their own. He felt if he were led blindfolded into a house he'd been in before, he would be able to identify the house from its distinct smell and ambience.

A roll of thunder rumbled, pulling him out of his musing; a loud crack of lightning flashed against the dark night sky, bathing the studio in an eerie light. The storm that had been brewing all evening was about to break wide open. He'd best hurry downstairs if he wanted to retrieve the evening paper from the front lawn before the coming rain.

Hurrying downstairs, he opened the front door and sprinted outside. Kashka streaked past him to get inside a heartbeat ahead of the raindrops while he made a mad dash for the rolled newspaper.

"Inventory..." Nicholas muttered, not looking forward to an evening alone. Especially not this kind of evening, the kind best spent under the covers, making love orchestrated by the fury of the storm raging outside. He tossed the newspaper onto the library sofa and went to the kitchen to rustle up something to share with Kashka.

"Do you believe the sorry state of things when I've been supplanted by inventory?" he complained to Kashka, putting down a saucer of milk to keep the cat occupied while he made tuna salad for two.

Kashka began lapping up the saucer of warm milk, seeming not to care a whit about her master's sad romantic plight.

"Well, see if I order anchovies on your half of the pizza next time," Nicholas told her.

When he'd finished making the tuna salad, Nicholas toasted some bread to make a sandwich for himself and put the leftover tuna into a small bowl for Kashka. Carrying both to the library with Kashka meowing underfoot, he set the cat's dinner upon the floor and his own upon the table in front of the sofa.

When he'd settled himself on the sofa, he took a bite of his sandwich, then opened the newspaper, scanning the headlines before turning to check on the art gallery happenings.

"Listen to this..." Nicholas began, talking to the cat, who continued to ignore him. "It says here that—"

Kashka having finished her dinner, interrupted him by jumping onto the coffee table and eyeing his dinner. "Oh, no, forget it. You already had your dinner." Nicholas made a shooing motion with his hand.

Kashka just sat there, unblinking.

She blinked a moment later when a giant pop of lightning plunged the house into total darkness. Shrieking, she leaped straight into Nicholas's lap.

"What happened to Ms. Aloof Cat?" Nicholas asked with a chuckle as he stroked the mewing feline. "Come on, we'll light some candles," he said soothingly, carrying her with him to the kitchen for matches.

"Ouch!" Nicholas swore a moment later in the darkness when he banged his shin on a piece of furniture. "Why didn't you warn me, Kashka? You're the one who can see in the dark."

Once in the kitchen, Nicholas set Kashka down while he made a search, drawer by drawer, for matches. Finally feeling the box, he carried it with him to the library and began lighting candles.

The French doors rattled in the wind and rain pinged against the glass as he walked around the room. Shaking out the match, he turned to see Kashka had returned to the library and helped herself to his sandwich.

At that moment she sat beside his plate, licking her paws in a show of unconcern.

"Lucky for you, you have nine lives," Nicholas said, advancing on her. Just then the telephone rang, interrupting Nicholas's playful advance, and the cat scooted away.

Returning to the kitchen, Nicholas picked up the phone on the sixth ring.

"I'll be right over," he said after Ali had told him water was leaking into her shop from the hole in the roof he'd repaired. The wind must have blown the weak shingles loose again.

"Don't wait up," he called to Kashka, who had disappeared, probably to the scene of her crime.

Backing his sports car out of the garage, he made his way through the rain-puddled streets, the thunder and lightning easing off in the waning storm. By the time he reached Ali's shop the rain had stopped completely.

The dash from his car to her door only left his feet wet.

She was waiting for him, opening the door and stepping aside to allow him entrance.

"Sorry to get you out in such terrible weather. I didn't know what to do and I was afraid a lot of damage might be done if the rain kept up like it was."

"Don't be sorry. I'm in favor of anything that tears you away from inventory."

"The inventory is finished."

"Good. Does that mean I can stay a while?"

"If you fix the leak," Ali said, following him upstairs.

"First things first," Nicholas said, pulling her into his arms, and capturing her arms behind her. "Now that the rain has stopped, the leak can wait to be fixed."

"What are you doing?" Ali had to laugh.

"Taking care of a little unfinished business," he said, brushing her lips with a kiss. "It's my turn now."

"Your turn? What are you talking about?"

"Truth or dare... remember? You went first, but I never got my turn. Are you ready?"

"I don't know—am I?"

"You'd better be. I'm about to pop the question." His eyes were suddenly serious, searching hers with dark intensity. "Ali, will you marry me?"

"Nicholas! Don't play games with me."

"So then you'd rather take the dare?" he asked, his eyes shuttered.

"What's the dare?" she asked, uncertain if he were serious.

He whispered into her ear.

"*That?*"

He nodded.

"In that case my answer is yes. Yes, I'll marry you, Nicholas."

"I was hoping you'd say that, you know," he said, smiling widely; he picked her up.

"What are you doing?" she demanded once again.

Ignoring her question, he carried her into the bathroom and set her down. "Why, I'm surprised at you, Ali. I thought a debutante would know all the rituals about weddings. Surely you've heard every bride-to-be gets a shower...." He reached to turn on the water.

"I don't think..." Ali said as the water began spraying, "that you have exactly the right understanding of the ritual." She giggled when he began to undo her buttons.

"Says who...?"

"Not me!" Ali exclaimed when his lips claimed a pebbled nipple with a warm, sexy kiss.

Their game was interrupted by the piercing wail of a siren.

"What's that?" Ali asked, pulling back.

"I don't know..." Nicholas said, listening intently. "Wait, it sounds like a fire engine siren. It's heading in this direction. There must be a fire nearby."

Nicholas turned off the shower, while Ali raced to look out the window.

"Good heavens!"

"What...? What is it?" Nicholas asked, reaching her side.

"Look at those flames! They're already blazing above the treetops."

"It must be one of the mansions along the river."

"Oh, Nicholas... you don't think..."

"Come on, let's go," he said, grabbing her hand and helping her back into her blouse.

She had the blouse buttoned by the time they went out the door and climbed into his sports car. The fire truck whizzed past at full throttle and they pulled out after it.

Within minutes Ali's stomach began to sink. It became obvious that the Knight mansion was indeed going up in flames.

"Stay in the car," Nicholas ordered, getting out.

"Where's Kashka?"

"She's probably already out. I'll see what I can discover and be right back." With that he headed toward a fireman who was hooking up a hose to a fire hydrant.

The fire chief waylaid him. "Up to your old tricks again, eh, Knight?"

"What?"

"You don't fool me. I know a firebug when I see one. At least you're smarter'n your old man. You knew to get out before you got trapped."

"I didn't set this fire."

"Then who did?"

"I don't know, but I was with..." Nicholas turned to point to Ali, but she wasn't there.

He swore.

"What is it?" the fire chief asked.

"It's Ali. She's gone in after the cat."

"Is that how you intend to explain away a woman's body in this fire, sonny? It won't work...this time...."

Nicholas's fist connected with the older man's jaw, knocking him to the ground. "There's a woman inside, damn you, and I'm going to get her out. Stay out of my way."

With that Nicholas took off at a full run toward the blazing inferno, peeling off his sweater and dipping it into a mud puddle on the way, praying all the while that Ali hadn't been crazy enough to go in after Kashka and knowing all the while she had done just that.

He reached the front door and yanked it open, but was met with a wall of flames that pushed him back, knocking him to his knees. Getting up, he ran around the house until he reached the French doors of the library.

Pushing against one of the doors, Nicholas fell into the smoke-filled room, where flames licked everywhere with demon greed.

"Ali!" he called. He had to find her. How could she have been so stupid as to act on impulse like that, threatening her life? *"Ali!"*

"Me-ow..."

"Kashka?" A timber fell nearby, spraying sparks that singed his hair.

He heard it again. "Me-ow...meow..."

Following the sound, Nicholas held his wet sweater to his face, keeping low so he could breathe.

"Me-ow..."

And then he saw them. Ali lay slumped in the fireplace with Kashka tight in her arms. Ali was awake but was clearly too frightened to move.

"Thank heaven...." Nicholas almost choked as he spoke, throwing the sweater over her face and dragging her and the cat across the room, dodging falling sprays of flame and cringing at the sound of the chandelier crashing in the hall. Punching open the door he'd used earlier, he cut his hand, but managed to get them outside, where a fire fighter arrived to drag them to safety.

"Don't ever scare me like that again," Nicholas said, wiping Ali's tear- and soot-streaked face. "What were you thinking? You could have been killed."

"I could hear Kashka meowing.... I had to save her...." Ali started to cry. "But then I..." She sniffed, then continued. "Then I panicked and I couldn't move...."

"That's okay, you're safe now, ma'am," the fire fighter said, giving her water.

Ali took a drink, then her eyes grew wide. "But your paintings, Nicholas...!"

"Forget the paintings.... I can paint again, but if I'd lost you I couldn't have gone on."

The fire chief came walking up as Kashka sat licking her sooty fur.

"You should have thought about that before you set the fire," the fire chief said, insistent that history was repeating itself.

"I told you, I didn't start the fire."

"Yeah? Then how did it start? There's no sign of a lightning strike."

"I don't know. I was having dinner and then the power went out, so I lit some candles. Ali called to tell me her roof was leaking, so I left to—"

"But didn't you know?" Ali asked, looking at Nicholas with sudden insight.

"Know what, ma'am?" the fire inspector asked.

"About Kashka. She's fascinated by fire. Whenever I'd light my fire, she'd sit by it for hours, watching it. She must have either knocked over the candle or batted the newspaper into the flame."

Nicholas felt the blood drain from his face.

"What? What is it?" Ali asked.

"Kashka was Camilla's kitten. I gave her to Camilla as a gift."

"Was Kashka with Camilla the night of the first fire?" Ali asked.

"She was always with Camilla. Like she is with you. And Camilla always burned scented candles in her bedroom."

"Nicholas..."

"It *was* an accident, after all, wasn't it? All these years I thought madness ran in my family, and now..." Nicholas pulled Ali into his arms.

"Well I'll be damned," the fire chief said.

Epilogue

"HURRY, OR WE'LL BE LATE for our own engagement party and the opening of your gallery," Ali coaxed, peeking into the small bathroom where Nicholas was shaving.

She paused to watch him brush the lather across his lean jaw with his old-fashioned shaving brush and inhaled the masculine fragrance of the shaving cream.

They'd lived together above her shop while the architect was drawing up plans for the new house on the Knight Hawthorne property. Thank goodness for the insurance money.

Her parents had arrived home from their European trip only a few days ago and had yet to meet the man who'd stolen their daughter's heart. Ali had thought news about the success of Attic Treasures enough of a surprise.

But it had been she who had been surprised at her father's pride in her accomplishment. Of course, he'd wanted to start a chain of Attic Treasures immediately, but she'd convinced him she liked things exactly as they were. To distract him she'd mentioned she'd met a man.

He hadn't exactly been thrilled when she'd told him that Nicholas was an artist. But when she'd assured him Nicholas didn't wear an earring or ride a motorcycle, he'd relaxed a little.

Still, she was nervous.

"Ouch!" A spot of red appeared in the white shaving cream where Nicholas had nicked himself.

"Want me to kiss it and make it better?" Ali asked, a note of laughter in her voice.

"I thought you wanted to get to this shindig on time," Nicholas answered. "But if you want to kiss it and make it all better, be my guest...." He undid the towel around his lean hips as he spoke.

"Nicholas!"

Ali ducked out of the bathroom to the rich sound of his laughter. She loved hearing him laugh.

Five minutes later he was done shaving and joined her in getting dressed. He zipped her red-beaded dress and she tied his tuxedo tie, all of which led to a bit of heavy petting that got them to the party fifteen minutes late.

Jessica waylaid them immediately.

"Well, what do you think, Nicholas? Isn't this going to be a lovely shop for your gallery?" she asked, indicating the expanse of white walls in the shop adjoining Attic Treasures.

"Too bad there aren't any paintings to hang yet," he said, arching a brow. "I think you two have jumped the gun on this gallery business."

"Nonsense. Ali and I are determined to see you become a famous artist."

"Well, then, why don't you let the boy hang his paintings in my chain of delis?" suggested the tall, distinguished-looking gentleman who joined them.

"Oh, Daddy."

"Sounds like a fine idea to me, Mr. Charbonneau," Nicholas said, extending his hand.

"You two *would* get along," Ali said with a sigh, wondering why she'd ever thought it a good idea that they should. "Daddy, this is Nicholas Knight . . . Nicholas . . . Daddy."

"Young man," Ali's father said, shaking the offered hand.

"Daddy, Nicholas is thirty-five."

"Well, that's a young man, isn't it?" her father said, looking to Jessica.

Caroline Farnsworth and Billy Lawrence joined them at that moment, and Caroline asked to see Ali's square-cut emerald engagement ring.

"It's beautiful, Ali. Isn't it beautiful, Billy?"

"Yeah, nice," Billy said in a bored voice.

"Where's Mother?" Ali asked, looking around the crowded shop.

"She's over with my mother," Caroline explained, rolling her eyes. "That's why I escaped over here. They've both got wedding brain."

"Excuse me, will you?" Billy said, wandering toward a nearby corner and a redhead in a backless dress.

"That reminds me. I've got something for you, Caroline," Nicholas said, pulling a long, slender, velvet box from his tuxedo jacket.

"For me?"

"Yes. When I sold Knight's Antiques, the dealer who bought it put me on to this. Consider it an engagement gift from Ali and me."

Caroline took the dark blue box from him and looked at Ali, who shrugged her surprise.

"What is it?"

"Well, open it and find out," Joe Allen said, joining them.

"It's exquisite!" Caroline squealed and reached to hug Ali and Nicholas. "I've never seen an antique hat pin like this before."

"Glad you like it," Nicholas said, squeezing Ali, who was smiling up at him.

"Are you ready, doll?" Joe asked Jessica.

"You two aren't leaving, are you?" Ali asked. "The party is just getting started."

"It's time we got started," Joe said, pointing to his watch with uncharacteristic concern.

"Want to tell them, Joe?" Jessica asked.

"Naw, you go right ahead, Jessica."

"Joe and I are eloping tonight," Jessica said, looking like a schoolgirl.

"Jessica!" Ali shrieked. "I don't believe it!"

"How fun," Caroline cried. "Wonder how Billy would feel about eloping. Mother is being such a pain about this wedding business. I swear she's planning to invite the whole world. Where *is* Billy, anyway?" she asked, glancing around.

The small group tried hard not to notice that Billy was in the midst of some heavy-duty flirting with the encouraging redhead.

"Excuse me, would you, please," Caroline said, lifting a glass of champagne from a waiter's tray.

"Where are you two going?" Ali's father asked. "I may be trying to talk Ali and this boy into it if I don't get my wife away from Caroline's momma soon."

"Daddy..."

"We're going to Vegas."

"Yes, she wanted a gambling stake instead of an engagement ring—'course, I don't know where she'd put a ring if I gave her one," Joe said, eyeing Jessica's bejeweled hand.

"I'll find a place for a ring. Come along," Jessica said, pulling Joe toward the door.

"Good luck," Ali called, waving good-bye.

At that moment Billy Lawrence let out a yell of indignation.

"What was that?" Ali asked.

"I think Caroline just broke her engagement with a hat pin," Nicholas said, trying to look innocent...and knowing he'd failed miserably when Ali broke into delighted laughter.

"I'm going to get your mother. Wait right here," Ali's father instructed.

"It's a shame all your new paintings burned in the fire, so we weren't able to hang some of them for the gallery opening tonight," Ali said, taking a sip of champagne.

"I don't know. I'd say it's a good thing the nude I painted of you burned—your father looks like a pretty tough customer. He'd probably have torn me limb from limb if I had hung it."

"Well, you wouldn't have hung that in public, would you?"

"Sure, I would have. I'm proud of you."

"That's lovely, but . . ."

"In fact, later tonight I thought maybe we could work on some poses. . . ."

Ali's father approached with her mother in tow. "There you are!" her father exclaimed. "I'm glad you stayed put, Ali. I'd never have found you again in this crush. I've finally got hold of your mother. Darling, this is our new son-in-law-to-be, Nicholas Knight."

"Pleased to meet you, Mrs. Charbonneau."

"Ali, he's quite handsome."

"I already told Ali the boy's a lot like me," her husband said with a pleased look that was starting to annoy Ali just the tiniest bit.

"Daddy . . ."

"How was your trip to Europe, Mrs. Charbonneau?"

"Expensive on shoe leather," Ali's father chimed in. "This woman dragged me through every cemetery in Europe, I swear. Her and her ancestor mania. Luckily I got a reprieve when we hit pay dirt in a churchyard in England."

"Why's that?" Nicholas asked.

"Mother must have found some trace of her mother's family," Ali said. "The family tree is top-heavy with Daddy's side."

"Why, dear, you're right, I did. I finally found out my grandmother's maiden name."

"What was it?" Ali asked.

"Hawthorne. Her name was Millicent Hawthorne. Isn't that a lovely name?"

HARLEQUIN® Temptation®

the Fortune Boys

A funny, sexy miniseries from bestselling
author Elise Title!

**LOSING THEIR HEARTS MEANT
LOSING THEIR FORTUNES...**
If any of the four Fortune brothers were unfortunate
enough to wed, they'd be permanently divorced from
the Fortune millions—thanks to their father's last will
and testament.

**BUT CUPID HAD OTHER PLANS FOR
DENVER'S MOST ELIGIBLE BACHELORS!**
Meet Adam in #412 **ADAM & EVE** (Sept. 1992)
Meet Peter in #416 **FOR THE LOVE OF PETE**
  (Oct. 1992)
Meet Truman in #420 **TRUE LOVE** (Nov. 1992)
Meet Taylor in #424 **TAYLOR MADE** (Dec. 1992)

**WATCH THESE FOUR MEN TRY TO WIN AT
LOVE AND NOT FORFEIT $$$**

HARLEQUIN®

Temptation

COMING NEXT MONTH

#409 THE KNIGHT IN SHINING ARMOR
JoAnn Ross

Rebels & Rogues, Book 9
Dash MacKenzie was no hero. But when he went undercover
to investigate beautiful, vulnerable Claren Wainwright, he
saw she needed a protector. Only would she want him
once she'd discovered the shocking truth?

#410 ASK DR. KATE Vicki Lewis Thompson

Dr. Kate Newberry *knew* there'd be trouble when her
book hit the stands. *Getting the Sex You Need from Your
Man* made her sound like some sex-starved aggressive
female—Kate was anything but. But try convincing wary
Garth Fredericks of that!

#411 HOT ARCTIC NIGHTS Ramona Bradly

Denali Park, Alaska, was the *last* place Charlie Madison,
efficiency expert and California girl, wanted to be in
midwinter. Especially when ranger Linc Tyler kept giving
her the deep freeze. Charlie was a threat to Linc's
livelihood—and to his libido.

#412 ADAM & EVE Elise Title

The Fortune Boys, Book 1
To protect his four sons from the wiles of women, tycoon
Alexander Fortune dictated in his will that if *any* of his
sons was foolish enough to marry, he'd lose his
inheritance. Adam Fortune thought he'd have no
problems remaining a bachelor. That is, until he met
lovely, luscious Laura....